# Past Praise for Alane Adams

### For the *Legends of Orkney* series

The *Legends of Orkney* series has won over 11 awards and finalist titles, including 2017 Moonbeam Children's Book Awards: Gold Medal, Best Book Series—Chapter Book

### For the *The Red Sun:*

"Percy Jackson meets Norse mythology in this captivating and unique adventure."
—*Foreword Reviews* (4 stars out of 5)

"*The Red Sun* is a roller coaster ride of adventure, Norse mythology, magic and mayhem. Between Sam facing awesome villains in the magical realm of Orkney to teachers turning into lizards, I had the best time doing the voiceover for the audiobook. Don't miss out on this terrific story!"
—Karan Brar, actor on Disney's *Jessie* and *Bunk'd*

"Alane Adams weaves , filled with magic and may in the *Legends of Orkney* ments of Norse mythology nd her young protagonist, Sam, on a unique quest to find himself and to save the entire realm of Orkney in the process."
—*Clarion*

"Gorgeously written, *The Raven God* delivers a fresh, lively fantasy with enough twists and turns to keep a young reader captivated. Sam, Mavery, and Perrin, tasked with saving Odin, make for delightful heroes. Set against magical ships, powerful witches, and determined armies, the three must summon both courage and smarts if they are to reach their goal. In the end, the three discover that the power of friendship is perhaps the greatest weapon of all. A magical read filled with other-worldly beings both good and evil—and always entertaining."

—Jennifer Gooch Hummer, award-winning author of *Girl Unmoored* and *Operation Tenley*

# The Blue Witch

Published by SparkPress, a BookSparks imprint,
A division of SparkPoint Studio, LLC
Tempe, Arizona, USA, 85281
www.gosparkpress.com

Published 2018
Printed in the United States of America
ISBN: 978-1-943006-77-9 (pbk)
ISBN 978-1-63152-461-5 (e-bk)

Library of Congress Control Number: 2018954280

Illustrations by Jonathan Stroh
Interior design by Tabitha Lahr

Witches of Orkney
Volume One:

THE BLUE WITCH

ALANE ADAMS

For Maddux

Quicksand Bogs

Balfour I·

Omera Aerie

Jadewick

Tarkana Fortress

Swamps

and

Orkney

# The
# WITCH'S CODE

My witch's heart is made of stone

Cold as winter, I cut to the bone

My witch's soul is black as tar

Forged in darkness to leave a scar

My witch's blood, it burns with power

Cross me not or you will cower

My witch's hands will conjure evil

I plot and plan, I'm quite deceitful

My witch's tongue will speak a curse

To bring you misery and so much worse

# Prologue

The two riders raced through woods shrouded in mist and hanging moss. Odin, the most powerful god in all of Asgard, urged his steed Sleipnir on. Sleipnir's eight legs pounded the ground sounding like drumbeats. Wind whipped at Odin and the woman gripping his waist.

Vor, Goddess of Wisdom, spoke in Odin's ear. "Hurry," she urged.

"Sleipnir can't see."

Vor whispered a string of words and the clouds above them parted, allowing the full moon to light the way. Odin clucked to Sleipnir until the thunder of hooves was deafening.

A burst of blinding green light led them to a clearing where a cloud of acrid smoke hung.

"We're too late," Odin said.

A black-haired woman wearing a heavy cloak lay sprawled on the forest floor. Odin took in the burn marks and deep scoring of claws that marred the trees. A battle had taken place here.

Odin helped Vor down. The seer's pale blonde hair flowed in a curtain down her back. Her sightless eyes were milky white, yet she saw more than any other being in Asgard.

She knelt by the woman, checking for signs of life, then shook her head.

A baby let out a wail.

Odin searched for the source of the noise, parting a swath of bushes. Tucked into the nook of a hollow trunk lay a babe swaddled in a blanket. A glowing bubble of energy encircled her. He waved his hand, wiping away the protective field, and lifted the child.

The baby fretted, reaching up to grab Odin's beard. He gently pried her fingers away and held her out.

"Well?"

Vor placed a hand on the baby's head, then nodded. "This is the child I saw in my vision."

A heavy weight settled on Odin as he cradled the child. *And so it begins.*

"She can't stay with us," Vor said softly. "When the other gods find out what she is, they will banish her."

Vor spoke true. The witches were the least liked of any creature in Odin's nine realms. Long ago, an ancient he-witch named Rubicus had cursed the sun and nearly destroyed every living thing. His daughter, Catriona, had carried on his vengeance, waging war with mankind until Odin had no choice but to rid mankind's world of magic forever.

The benevolent king of Orkney, Hermodan, had offered part of his kingdom as sanctuary, a handful of islands that Odin could lift from earth and cast into the Ninth Realm. Every magical thing, creature, stick, and stone had gone with it, including the witches. Odin would have left the hateful witches behind to lose their powers forever, but Hermodan had believed there was some good to be found in them.

Odin smiled down at the babe. She had fallen asleep in his arms. Downy raven hair covered her head.

*Poor thing.* Too young to have already suffered so much loss.

He looked at Vor, deciding. "I will send her to the Tarkana Creche. She is one of them. They will see to her upbringing."

Vor grimaced. "They will turn her into a witch."

"She is already a witch."

"I mean they'll turn her into one of *them*, a heartless cold fish."

The babe opened her eyes, giving Odin a sleepy smile. Emerald eyes stared back at him. But in the center of her pupils there was a spark, like a shining star. Something hopeful stirred in him.

"Perhaps she'll be the one to change the witches," he said.

Vor's face softened. "Time will tell. Who will take her to them? The witches despise you; don't put that on her."

Odin whistled softly, and a small green-furred creature emerged from the trees. It had long floppy ears, almond-shaped eyes, and spindly limbs. It scampered across the clearing and dropped into a low bow.

"Yes, Your Highest?"

Odin placed the babe in the furry creature's arms. "Fetch, I am entrusting this child to you. Take her to the Tarkana Creche and leave her with a witch named Old Nan. She has a soft spot in her cold heart."

Fetch nodded, bowing low before scurrying off with the baby.

"Do you think she will be safe?" Vor asked.

Odin watched them go with a pang. "The prophecy has begun. Until it is completed, we are all in great danger."

# Chapter 1

Abigail marched toward the iron gates of the Tarkana Fortress, holding her chin high. She wasn't going to cry, not today, even though Old Nan had tied her braids so tight her scalp stung.

The Creche wasn't her home anymore.

The other girls had been fawned over by proud mothers as they gathered their things and tried on crisp new uniforms.

Abigail had sat on her bed, waiting quietly.

Honestly, it didn't bother her that she didn't have a mother. A witch didn't have much use for one.

Newborn witchlings were left at the Creche to be raised by lesser witches like Old Nan. Mothers visited three times a year: once on Promotion Day, again on a girl's birthday, and a special visit on Yule Day, when they would bring a small gift and drink cinnamon cocoa by the fire.

Those days, Abigail hid in the shadows, watching as the other witchlings glowed under the attention of these strange and powerful creatures.

At age nine, witchlings were sent off to the famed Tarkana Witch Academy, inside the coven's walled fortress, to be trained in the art of witchery.

She came to a stop outside the entrance, gripping her small valise in one hand. Gloomy clouds had gathered in a knot overhead. Her new uniform itched her neck, and she tugged at the collar.

All she had to do was take two steps, and she would be inside the gates and on her way to becoming a great witch.

She tried to slide her foot forward, but it stubbornly remained stuck in place.

A pair of girls rushed past, practically flying through the open gates.

Glaring down at her foot, Abigail whispered, "Don't be a silly droopsy-daisy. Today is a new beginning."

Her foot wavered in the air like a dowsing rod, but before she could take the step, someone shoved her to the ground.

"Outta my way!" a stout-faced witchling bellowed. A lanky girl skulked alongside her.

Glorian and Nelly. The two were part of a trio that stuck together like tree sap in summer. Which meant . . .

Yep.

Behind them, a girl sailed along with her nose in the air as if she were royalty. Endera. The most horrible witchling in the entire Tarkana coven.

Endera paused to smile sweetly down at Abigail. "Aren't you clumsy as a blind sneevil?"

The other girls snickered, and the trio swept on through the gates.

Abigail picked pebbles out of her torn stockings, biting back tears. They had been friends once, she and Endera, but something had changed. Now, Endera treated Abigail as if she were worm dust.

Abigail stood, gripping her valise, and started limping toward the gates, when a rumbling growl made the hair on the back of her neck stand up.

Turning her head to the side, she spied something rustling in the bushes. Something large and hairy. She could just make out a pair of eyes watching her—dark eyes that glowed with malice.

Her throat went dry. She couldn't move. If she took another step, she was certain that thing would pounce on her.

And then a stern woman with a pointed chin appeared at the gate, beckoning Abigail with long fingers.

"Move it along, child, or you'll find yourself locked out until next year."

The thing in the bushes quietly retreated, and Abigail could breathe again. She quickly moved inside the gates.

A throng of chattering witchlings, all clutching suitcases, was assembled in a courtyard in front of an imposing gray building with GREAT HALL carved into its headstone. Across the courtyard, an overgrown garden invited exploring with pebble-lined walking paths that wound through the mass of brambles and trees.

Next to the Great Hall, a bronzed sign announced the Tarkana Academy, a maze of low buildings with arched corridors lined with classrooms. Older witchlings hung out of open doors, whispering and staring at the new girls.

The stern witch who had bidden Abigail inside climbed the steps of the Great Hall. She turned at the top, her gaze moving slowly over each of them. Silence spread as the girls waited for her to speak.

"Welcome, firstlings. I am Madame Vex, headmistress. Make no mistake, this is not the Creche. You will not be coddled here. We have assembled the finest teachers to instruct you in the art of witchery. Do well, and you will move on. Fail to impress, and you will be sent back to the Creche."

Her eyes fell on Abigail, lingering.

Abigail swallowed the lump in her throat as Madame Vex went on.

"The witchling with the highest marks on Yule Day will be named Head Witchling of her class, a great honor that I myself once claimed. Now, before you meet your teachers, let us go over the rules. Rule number one: no running, ever. It is unbecoming a witch. Rule number two: never go into the swamps outside these walls without permission. A wandering girl could get lost, or worse. Rule number three: no one is allowed into the dungeons. They have been closed for centuries and are overrun with hungry rathos."

She stepped to the side, and behind her, four witches of varying ages marched out of the shadows of the Great Hall.

Madame Vex extended her arm. "Madame Barbosa will instruct you in your ABCs— Animals, Beasts, and Creatures."

Madame Barbosa wore a flowing gown of multicolored stripes. Her face had a feline look, with high cheekbones and slanted eyes. She flared her skirts out and dipped in a half curtsy.

Madame Vex moved on to a bone-faced woman with not an ounce of cheer.

"Madame Arisa will be your Spectacular Spells instructor."

Madame Arisa sniffed a greeting and then snapped her fingers, disappearing in a cloud of purplish smoke.

The witchlings all gasped.

Up next was a plump witch with a wide stripe of white running through her raven hair.

"Madame Radisha will be teaching you Positively Potent Potions," Madame Vex announced.

"Welcome, witchlings, welcome." Madame Radisha waved her hands in the air. Her fingers were covered in dazzling gemstone rings.

Last was a wizened hag bent over nearly double. Gnarled hands rested on a four-legged contraption strung with the bones of tiny animals.

"The History of Witchery will be taught by our eldest member, Madame Greef."

The old witch bobbed her head, baring blackened gums in a toothless smile.

The headmistress turned back to the girls and clapped her hands. "Pair up and find a partner to room with. Madame Radisha will escort you to the dormitory. You have one hour to unpack and then assemble in the Dining Hall."

"Quickly girls, find a match," Madame Radisha trilled.

Witchlings scrambled, linking arms and pairing up. Abigail hunted for a friendly face. She spied Minxie, a cross-eyed girl who had sometimes eaten lunch with her back at the Creche.

Abigail waved and Minxie began to raise her hand, but Endera stepped in between, shoving Minxie toward another witchling.

Abigail let her hand drop. The lawn cleared until she was the only girl left.

Madame Radisha put an arm around her shoulder.

"Lucky you, the odd girl out gets the attic room," she said brightly. "Perfect fit for one, and you don't have to share."

She marched Abigail over to the dormitory tower, a tall round building with bands of ivy wrapped around gray stone.

They ducked through a low door and entered the main room. Bookshelves crammed with thick tomes lined the walls. A couple of low sofas and tables were occupied by older girls studying. In the center of the room, a narrow set of spiral stairs led to the upper floors.

"Top of the stairs, dear, you can't miss it." Madame Radisha gave Abigail a gentle shove.

Abigail dragged her valise up floor after floor, ignoring the giggling girls who ran room to room, shouting out dibs.

At the top, she pushed open a narrow door. The room was dusty and lined with cobwebs. It held a small iron bed, a rickety desk, and a pile of bedding.

She set her valise down and began to unpack, thinking about that beast in the shrubs. It might have been a Shun Kara. The fearsome black wolves roamed the woods on Balfour Island.

Thankfully, she was safe inside the walls of the Tarkana Fortress. Nothing could get to her in here.

# Chapter 2

Abigail glumly swirled the spoon around her bowl of porridge. Two weeks into the term and she still hadn't made a single friend. It was like she had some kind of contagious disease. If a witchling so much as glanced Abigail's way, Endera found a way to scare her off.

A shadow fell over her. She looked up with a hopeful smile then let it drop.

"That's my seat," Endera said.

"That's right. It's her seat, so shove off," Glorian said.

"Or else I'll be peeling your eyeballs loose," Nelly added, waggling skinny fingers tipped with sharpened nails.

Abigail looked around the Dining Hall. There were two other empty tables. "There's plenty of space, Endera."

"That's not the point. You're sitting in my spot."

Abigail sighed. She could argue, or she could move. She got up, lifting her tray, and headed for an open table, but Endera stuck her foot out. Abigail went flying, landing facedown in her bowl of porridge.

Anger rippled through her, sending strange tingles of energy down to her fingertips and toes. The other girls giggled as she got to her feet. Sticky bits of oats spattered her face.

Endera opened her mouth, probably to flap on about how Abigail was clumsy as a blind sneevil.

Before she could think better of it, Abigail grabbed the glass of milk off Endera's tray and dumped it over the girl's head. White liquid dripped down Endera's hair and onto her face, soaking her dress.

"I'm going to destroy you," Endera swore.

Abigail did the only smart thing. She ran.

She flung open the door to the courtyard and dashed down the first garden path she found. Her feet flew so fast, her pigtails stuck out straight behind her.

This was breaking one of Madame Vex's big rules—no running ever—but Abigail didn't dare slow down. She rounded the curved path that led to the back of the gardens and skidded to a stop.

Endera stood blocking her way. Damp clumps of hair hung over her eyes as she glared at Abigail. Her two cronies stood by her side. Glorian cracked her knuckles loudly, while Nelly waggled her sharpened nails.

Abigail took a step back. "We're even now, Endera. So just leave me alone."

"Who's going to make me? You?" Endera laughed, and Nelly and Glorian joined in, snorting like a pair of sneevils.

Before Abigail could flee, Nelly grabbed her, wresting her arms behind her back. "Give her a blast of your witchfire," she urged.

"Yeah, singe off one of those braids she's so fond of," Glorian added, lifting one of Abigail's braids.

"What did I ever do to you?" Abigail cried, struggling to free herself. "We used to be friends."

Endera curled her lip. "Friends? I took pity on a motherless witchling with no one to visit her." She drew her hands in a circle, preparing to zap Abigail, when a strange voice called out.

"Stop!"

The witchlings froze.

The voice came from one of the towering jookberry trees that grew over the wall separating the Tarkana Fortress from the swamps. Red clumps of fruit hung down from the thick limbs.

Abigail shielded her eyes to see who it was. A boy clung to one of the branches. He was slender, with a sheaf of sandy brown hair that fell over a pair of glasses.

Endera threw her hands forward, waggling her fingers. A tiny trickle of green fire shot into the tree. The boy yelped and then lost his hold on the branch, arms flailing as he landed in a heap at Abigail's feet.

# Chapter 3

*T*his was bad.

Hugo picked himself up, spitting out bits of grass. If only he'd kept his big mouth shut, he wouldn't be stuck in the middle of a witch battle.

"Who are you?" the lead bully asked.

He brushed off his palms and pushed his glasses firmly into place. "My name is Hugo Suppermill. I order you to leave this girl alone or face the consequences."

The witchling sneered. "You're just a Balfin boy from town. You don't belong on Tarkana property, so get lost before I zap your ears off."

"Go on," the witchling next to him urged in a low voice. "I can handle them."

Hugo was fond of his ears, but he refused to be seen as a coward. Reaching into his pocket, he drew out the medallion he'd taken from his brother Emenor's coat pocket that morning.

The polished flint disc hung on a silver chain and was carved with strange symbols. Emenor claimed a witchling had given it to him and filled it with magic.

As a scientist-in-training, Hugo had been skeptical magic was real. He'd heard stories about the witches, of course, but he'd never actually seen magic up close. But ever since Hugo had scoffed at Emenor's claims, strange things had happened.

Like when Hugo had gone to turn in his Maths homework the next day, and the neatly penciled columns of numbers had vanished, as if an invisible eraser had wiped them clean. Hugo had tried writing his answers in ink, but the same thing had happened.

Now, Hugo was failing Maths, thanks to Emenor's trickery. But instead of being mad, Hugo was fascinated.

He had taken to hiding in the jookberry tree, listening in on witchlings practicing spells and writing everything down in his pocket journal. Someday he would understand the secret to how magic worked.

Gripping the chain, he swung the disc side to side. Emenor hadn't said how it worked exactly. Was it going to shoot out magic?

The trio of bullies stepped back, looking unsure. But when nothing happened, a smile came over their faces.

"Blast him," their leader said. The three witchlings raised their hands, drawing them in a circle, and muttered some words.

*Words.* That was it! He must need to say a spell. But which one? Hugo tried to recall his notes.

"Anytime," the witchling by his side muttered.

He said the first thing that came to him. "*Fein kinter, ventimus!*"

A jolt ran up his arm as a sharp wind came out of nowhere, and the trio of witches yelped as stinging gravel sprayed their faces.

Hugo stared, shocked that it had worked.

The witchling at his side grabbed his hand, crying, "Come on!"

She dragged him through the gate that led to the swamps. Behind them, shouts rang out as the other three gave chase. Stuffing the medallion in his pocket, Hugo broke into a run, trying to keep up with the witchling. She ran like a Shun Kara wolf was nipping at her heels.

After a few minutes, the shouts of their pursuers faded, and the witchling drew to a halt.

"Enough," she panted. "I can't run anymore."

Hugo put his hands on his knees, chest heaving as he caught his breath.

The jookberry trees were long gone, replaced by a canopy of gnarled branches and boggy ground. Black-winged shreeks flew overhead, diving and twisting as they hunted mice.

"Are you crazy?" the witchling said, turning to yell at him. "You used magic on a witch. She could have blasted you to bits!"

Hugo calmly wiped his glasses and put them back in place. "You have a point. My brother, Emenor, says curiosity can kill a cat, and I'm beginning to see how."

She gaped at him a moment and then folded her arms. "Are you always so honest?"

He nodded. "I can't help it. I'm a scientist—at least, I want to be one someday."

"Well, Hugo Suppermill, I'm Abigail Tarkana, and we're lost. I hope you know your way out of here."

"I think it's this way," he said, pointing at a faint glow of morning sun in a break in the trees.

They began to walk, hopping over the worst of the bogs.

Excitement gripped Hugo. He had a real live Tarkana witch to interview! Finally, he could get answers to his long list of questions.

"Is it confusing that every witch has the same last name?" he asked.

"No. Our coven is our family. Besides, all great witches are known by their first name. Catriona was the greatest of them all. She was my ancestor and someday, I'm going to be as powerful as she was."

Hugo frowned. "Then how come you didn't use magic to defend yourself?"

Abigail shrugged. "Against Endera? She's not worth it." But she looked away as she said it.

Hugo stopped to peer closely at her. "You're lying, which means. . ." His brain ticked over the facts and arrived at the only logical conclusion. "You don't have any magic, do you?"

"Do so." But two splotches of red spotted her cheeks.

"Then prove it." Hugo pulled out his journal from his back pocket. He slid out his pencil, licking the tip with his tongue. "Observation Number Seven: Abigail Tarkana Uses Magic."

Abigail's hands clenched at her sides. "You don't want to make me mad."

"Okay," Hugo said, pencil poised over the paper. "Go ahead then."

She raised her fists, waving them at him. "Watch out, Hugo Suppermill, or so help me, I will zap you where you stand."

He blinked. "Duly warned. Still waiting."

She threw her hands forward. Hugo cringed, but there was nothing. Zippo. Not a hint of the crackling green witchfire Endera had used on him.

Her face fell. "Who am I kidding? I don't have a drop of magic. I've been nine for months. That's when witches are supposed to get their first set of powers, but so far,

nothing's happened." She looked at him with frightened eyes. "What if I'm a glitch-witch?"

"Glitch-witch? What's that?"

"A witch who never gets her magic. Old Nan back at the Creche never got more than a smidgen of magic, barely enough to boil water."

"I'm sure your magic will come in when you're ready."

"Well, it had better come soon. We have our first exam in Spectacular Spells next week. If I can't call on my witchfire, Madame Arisa will fail me. Do you know what they do to witches who fail?"

Before Hugo could answer, a snuffling snort came from the shadows, followed by a sharp squeal.

"What. Was. That?" Abigail gulped out, grabbing his arm.

"Uh . . . I'm not sure. But logically speaking, it could be a sneevil."

Sneevils were Hugo's least favorite creature. The size of an overgrown pig, they had long curved tusks sharp enough to run right through a grown man.

"Then, logically speaking, we should run!" Abigail said.

# Chapter 4

Branches whipped at Abigail as they fled. She spied a thin spire from the Tarkana Fortress through the trees, and her heart lifted. The gate into the gardens must be just ahead. Next to her, Hugo cried out as he stepped into a hole and twisted his ankle.

He sank to the ground, grabbing at his calf. "Help! It's stuck!"

Abigail froze as a sneevil emerged from the bushes. Its ugly pig eyes glared out of slits over curved tusks that jutted from its lower jaw. Bristly hair covered mottled gray skin.

"Abigail, run!" Hugo shouted.

Running sounded like an excellent plan, but Hugo had stood up to Endera for her. She couldn't just leave him.

Two more even bigger sneevils joined the first. Grunts and snarls rumbled from their chests. They tossed their heads, showing off those wicked pointed tusks.

Hugo tugged on his ankle, but it was firmly stuck in the hole. "I can't get it out, Abigail. Just go. I can't bear the thought of you being hurt." A smudge of mud striped his cheek and his eyes pleaded with hers behind his glasses. "Please. You're the only friend I've got."

Abigail's heart melted. It was the nicest thing anyone had ever said to her.

Flipping her pigtails over her shoulders, she shook out her hands. It was time to take charge of her magic.

"I have an idea," she said. "Earlier, when Endera made me mad, I felt a tingle."

"You think it was your magic?"

"I don't know. But maybe if you make me mad, it'll come back."

"How do I do that?"

The sneevils lowered their snouts, digging in the dirt with their hooves as they readied to charge.

"Tell me I'm never going to be a great witch."

Hugo repeated the words. "You're never going to be a great witch."

"No, silly, you have to mean it."

He took a deep breath and shouted, "Abigail Tarkana is the worst witch in all of Orkney."

There. A spark kicked in her chest. The sneevils paused, looking around in confusion.

"Again," she said.

"She is never ever going to get her magic, and everyone will laugh at her, especially Endera."

Ooh, she hated it when Endera laughed at her. The spark ignited into a tiny flame. She ground her boot in the mud as the wild beasts warily inched closer.

"More," she said.

"Endera will always be the better witch, and you know it. She will be the most powerful witch of all time, and you will be her serving maid, bringing her tea and cookies."

That did it. The day Abigail served Endera tea was the day sneevils could fly.

She lifted her hands. "*Fein kinter*," she began, reciting the words she had learned in Madame Arisa's Spectacular Spells class. A faint whisper tickled her ears.

*I call on my magic.*

Hugo threw a dirt clod at the closest sneevil, driving it back a step. "We're out of time, Abigail. We need some witchfire."

"*Fein kinter*," she repeated with more confidence, drawing her hands in a circle.

A tiny spark leapt from her fingertips. She moved her hands faster and faster, feeling a charge build up inside her, and then thrust her palms forward. A sizzling jolt of energy shot up her arm as a trickle of arctic-blue witchfire zinged out of her palms straight for the closest sneevil.

It hardly dented its thick hide, serving instead to make it angrier. Its rumbling snarl grew louder as the other two stepped up on either side.

Suddenly, the sneevils froze, lifting their snouts in the air, and then they squealed, turning as one and fleeing.

Abigail dropped her arms in relief.

"What just happened?" Hugo said.

"I dunno. Maybe I scared them away."

She looked at her hands. Had she used magic?

"You just used magic," Hugo confirmed with an awed gasp.

"I guess I did," she said, but an uneasy feeling settled in as she studied her palms.

"But how come your witchfire is blue?" Hugo asked.

Abigail had no idea. Every witchling knew witchfire was emerald-green. Which meant there was something very off about her magic.

She knelt beside Hugo and tugged his foot loose. A branch snapped, as if something heavy had stepped on it. A menacing growl brought them to their feet as a beast stepped from the trees into the far side of the clearing.

It was taller than them, a massive wolf-like creature with hulking shoulders and a shaggy mane. Pointed ears stood at attention. Black eyes held a yellow slit in their center and slanted upward. Its paws were the size of dinner plates, tipped with lethal-looking claws that curled into the soil. It opened its jaws, revealing a row of razor-sharp teeth.

"Is that a Shun Kara?" Hugo asked.

"Shun Karas aren't that big."

"Can you blast it?"

She slid him a glance. "Seriously? My puny magic's not going to stop that."

"So, what do we do?"

An idea quickly hatched. The gate to the gardens was close. They just had to distract the creature long enough to get inside the fortress. She drew her hands up, charging her magic.

"Get ready to run."

The beast took a step closer, and Abigail directed her palms upward at a mass of dead branches overhead. She blasted witchfire at the rotted wood, causing the heavy branches to break loose. Too late, the beast looked up as the falling wood entangled it.

While it tore at the branches, they ran.

Fear clogged Abigail's throat as she raced behind Hugo. The iron gate came into view. She pushed Hugo in ahead of her and then jerked to a halt as jaws clamped down on the hem of her uniform. She frantically tugged on the skirt and ripped the fabric free. Before it could lunge again, Hugo pulled her inside and slammed the gate shut.

The beast gnashed the iron with its teeth, but the gate held fast. Finally, it turned away, casting one last snarl over its shoulder before slinking off into the woods.

Abigail sagged in relief.

"Are you all right? Did it hurt you?" Hugo asked, checking her from head to toe.

"No. I'm fine." Her heart rate slowly returned to normal. "I better get to class before Madame Vex notices I'm gone."

"Yeah. Me too." He bit his lower lip. "I've never skipped school before." He gave a faint smile. "Then again, I've never faced three sneevils and been chased by a wild beast."

She looked through the bars into the dense swamp. "You can't go that way. That thing could still be waiting."

"There's a service entrance on the other side of the gardens. I'll be fine." He gave a quick nod and then ducked into the bushes.

"It was nice to meet you," she called out.

He turned with a grin, his face framed in leaves. "Same here. So maybe I'll see you after school? We can try to get to the bottom of why your magic is blue."

"I'd like that."

He nodded, then disappeared from sight.

# Chapter 5

Abigail snuck into the Dining Hall as the other girls were finishing their lunch. If anyone asked why she'd missed her morning classes, she would simply say she'd had an upset stomach. Minxie tapped her on the shoulder.

"Here," she held out Abigail's book bag. "You left this behind this morning."

Abigail was about to thank her when the girl's eyes widened, and she fled.

"Abigail Tarkana!" a voice boomed. "I hope you have an explanation for why you missed Magical Maths this morning."

Abigail turned to see Madame Vex bearing down on her.

"Sorry, Madame Vex. I wasn't feeling well."

Madame Vex gasped. "Is that a tear in your uniform?" She pointed at the jagged rip in Abigail's skirt.

"Yes, ma'am." Abigail twitched the fabric out of sight. "Sorry. I took a walk in the gardens to get some air, and it snagged on a bush."

"That's a lie," Endera said, marching up with Glorian and Nelly at her side. "She went into the swamps. We saw her."

Madame Vex's eyes flared. "Is that true, Abigail?"

Abigail tried to think of something, *anything,* to say, but Glorian jumped in.

"It's true, Madame Vex. She wouldn't listen when we told her not to."

"Yeah," Nelly added, "she just barged out the gate and said the rules were *stuuupid.*" She waggled her hands as she said the last part.

Abigail groaned as Madame Vex's face turned bright red. The entire Dining Hall went silent as the teacher grabbed Abigail by the ear, pinching it painfully. "We will see what Madame Hestera has to say about that."

The girls let out excited oohs. Madame Hestera was the leader of the Tarkana coven and the most powerful witch alive.

Madame Vex marched Abigail out the Dining Hall and down a long corridor toward a towering set of double doors.

She was taking Abigail to the Great Hall, where the witches convened their councils. Abigail had never been inside, but she'd heard rumors spread by the older girls about a giant spider that lived there and ate witchlings who misbehaved.

The rest of her classmates trailed behind, eager to see what punishment awaited her. Madame Vex nodded briskly at the pair of Balfin guards dressed in black uniforms standing outside. They quickly opened the doors and stepped aside.

Madame Vex dragged her inside and finally released Abigail's ear. The doors swung shut behind them, locking out the disappointed gaggle of girls.

Abigail rubbed her ear to get the blood flowing again and looked around in awe.

Marble columns rose up to support high ceilings. Ornately woven tapestries hung on the stone walls. One of them showed a bearded man kneeling in front of a sun stitched with jagged streaks of red.

On the raised dais at the far end of the room, a gray-haired woman sat in a high-backed chair. Her black gown was buttoned to her neck. One hand rested on a cane, its knobby emerald tip just visible between her knuckles. A large black curtain hung behind the dais.

A pair of witches sat on either side of her, their superior air marking them as members of the High Witch Council. Abigail recognized Endera's mother, Melistra, from her visits to the Creche.

Melistra scared Abigail. She had overheard her yelling at Old Nan once, shaking one of the nursery's record books and reducing the poor woman to tears.

There was no sign of the spider, so maybe it *was* just a rumor.

Madame Vex stopped in front of the dais and bowed low. The headmistress elbowed Abigail, and she dropped into a clumsy curtsy.

"What is the meaning of this interruption?" Hestera demanded, pursing wrinkled lips.

"This witchling ran into the swamps even though she knew it was against the rules," Madame Vex reported.

"She did, did she?" Hestera's eyes narrowed as she studied the girl. "What's your name, child?"

"Abigail," she said, her voice barely a whisper. Her knees were shaking so badly she was afraid she was going to fall down.

"Who is your mother?" Hestera demanded.

"Her name was Penelope," Abigail dutifully answered.

Hestera frowned. "Penelope? I don't recall a witch by that name."

Before Abigail could explain that she had passed away shortly after Abigail was born, a hairy black appendage poked out from behind the curtains.

Hestera caught her gaze and gave a sly smile, clapping her hands sharply.

The curtain fell away, revealing a giant web that held a spider the size of a carriage. It was nimbly spinning more webbing as it moved. Red and yellow bands encircled each leg. It had a set of jaws that could swallow Abigail whole.

"Did you know the Tarkanas were named after this lovely creature?" Madame Hestera said, waving a hand at her pet. "We call her the Great Mother. Would you like to see her up close?"

Abigail shook her head, shifting her feet to take a step back.

Madame Vex clamped a hand on her shoulder, stopping her. "How should she be punished?"

"The child should be expelled," Melistra cut in, her voice like chipped ice. "She broke the rules."

Abigail fought back tears. Expelled? For running in the swamps?

Madame Vex cleared her throat. "It was her first infraction, Melistra. Surely not cause for her to be expelled."

Melistra started to argue, but Madame Hestera rapped her cane sharply on the dais. "Enough interruptions. Detention after school every day for a week."

Abigail's spirits sank. Detention every day? She wouldn't be able to meet Hugo, which meant she wouldn't get any answers to her strange witchfire.

"And I'll expect you to keep an eye about you, Madame Vex," Hestera added in a low voice. "With that

spy we caught snooping around, we can't be sure what Odin is up to."

Madame Vex bowed her head, backing away.

Abigail followed, looking over her shoulder one last time. Melistra's disdainful gaze locked on her, sending a frisson of fear up her spine.

Outside, the girls scattered as the door opened.

Madame Vex clapped her hands. "Come, girls, hurry along. You'll be late to Positively Potent Potions. You don't want Madame Radisha to mark you tardy."

The girls squealed, fleeing toward the classroom. Abigail started to follow when Madame Vex said, "Madame Arisa tells me you are failing Spectacular Spells—that your magic hasn't come in yet."

Abigail said nothing, afraid that if she lied, Madame Vex would know.

The headmistress sniffed. "Perhaps you will be expelled anyway." With those words, she waved Abigail off to class.

# Chapter 6

Black banners flapped in the parapets of the Balfin
School for Boys, a cheerless building built out of
weathered gray stone. From the inner courtyard
came the staccato sounds of students marching in rhythm.
They were always practicing drills to become soldiers.

There wasn't much else for a boy to do when he came
of age but join the Black Guard, the witches' private army.
It was that or become a blacksmith and make armor for
the Black Guard. Or work in the stables and tend the
horses for the Black Guard. Only a select few became part
of the Balfin Council, eligible as consorts for the witches.
Hugo had never understood why the witches needed such
a big army. There hadn't been a war in centuries.

He hurried around to the rear of the building and lifted
the root cellar door. Emenor bragged he snuck in and out
this way whenever he ditched school. The wooden steps
creaked loudly as he climbed down. The cellar smelled
earthy and slightly rotten. Bins of vegetables were stacked
up on the dirt floor. As Hugo pulled the trapdoor shut, a
voice spoke in the shadows.

"Give it back."

Hugo turned.

Emenor pushed himself off the wall, stalking toward him. His brother was tall and lanky. Dark hair fell over his forehead, hiding his eyes.

Hugo tugged the medallion out of his pocket and dropped it into Emenor's hand. The older boy rubbed it with his fingers, and his lip curled in anger.

"You used it, you little turnip." He grabbed Hugo, slamming him back against the wall. "Who said you could use my magic?"

"I'm sorry. It's just . . . I wanted to see how magic works, and there was this witch battle—"

"Witch battle? With who?"

"A witchling named Endera."

Emenor stepped back, looking frightened. "You used magic against Endera Tarkana? Have you lost your mind?"

"What's wrong?"

"Endera Tarkana is the daughter of a High Witch."

"So?"

"Don't you know anything about the witches? A High Witch is powerful—more powerful than you can imagine. We have to destroy this, or she'll track it back to me."

Emenor threw the medallion against the stone floor. There was a flash of green, and then it shattered into pieces.

He took Hugo by his collar and shook him. "You owe me another medallion, you hear me? Soon, or I'll be giving you a beating every day until you make it right." Shoving him aside, Emenor stomped up the set of stairs that led into the school.

Hugo leaned back against the cold bricks, trying to slow his heart down. He had never seen Emenor this mad before. His brother liked to boss him around, but deep down, he was usually an okay brother.

How was he going to get another magical medallion? Maybe Abigail would give him one if he explained why he needed it.

Hugo slowly followed Emenor up the stairs, ducking out the small door that opened into a corner of the busy kitchen and slipping out into the main hall. It was passing period, so the halls were crowded with boys. He hurried into his Ancient History class.

Professor Oakes was one of Hugo's favorite teachers and came from a high-ranking family. Like many of the Balfin elite, he kept his head clean-shaven and wore long black robes.

As Oakes droned on about long-ago witches, Hugo doodled on his paper. He drew the muscled shoulders of the beast, its broad head and slanted eyes.

Hugo read a lot, so he knew just about everything there was to know about the animals on Balfour Island, but he had never seen a creature like this before.

"Can anyone tell me why there are no he-witches left today? Mr. Suppermill?"

Hugo set his pencil down. "A he-witch named Rubicus tried to show Odin he was more powerful, so he cursed the sun to poison the land. It nearly destroyed Midgard, the realm of man. Odin had to cut off Rubicus's head to stop the curse."

Professor Oakes raised his eyebrows in surprise. "You've done your homework. But how did that lead to no more little he-witches?"

Hugo knew the answer well. "Odin was so angry at what Rubicus had done he cursed the witches to never have sons again."

Oakes nodded in approval. "But do you know what the Rubicus Prophecy says?"

Hugo shook his head. There hadn't been anything in the books about a prophecy.

"Allow me to tell the story." Oakes opened a tattered old book and began to read from it. "As the red sun burned like a blazing torch, Odin raised his mighty sword, Tyrfing, over the head of Rubicus. 'I take no pleasure in ending your life,' said Odin. 'But you went too far this time.' Then Rubicus vowed, 'You may take my head and end my life, but one day, I will be avenged. A son of mine will destroy all that you have built.' Odin became so enraged he swore a curse, 'Then never again shall a witch bear a male child.'"

"What did Rubicus do?" a boy up front asked.

"He laughed. Then he challenged Odin: 'Mark my words, not even a god as powerful as you can control the fates. One day, a daughter of my daughter's daughter will break the curse and bear a son to take my vengeance—" Oakes snapped the book shut. "And bring war to Orkney."

The room was silent, and then Hugo raised his hand.

"So his fate is not his to choose?" he asked.

Oakes frowned. "What do you mean?"

Hugo shrugged. "It just doesn't seem fair. I mean, what if this boy doesn't want to take vengeance and start a war?"

Oakes smiled. "He'll be a witch; of course, he'll want to go to war. It's in their blood."

"How come us Balfins don't have any magic?" a sullen boy named Gregor asked. A fringe of dark hair lined his brow. "Why do we have to serve the witches?"

"You think we are so powerless?" Oakes asked.

Gregor shrugged. "They're always bossing my dad around. He sews dresses for them, but he's not even allowed to speak when he's fitting them."

The professor paced in front of the class. "Think of the witches as a stallion—an animal powerful enough to stomp the life out of a small boy like you. Yet a trained stallion is easily controlled with just a touch of the reins." He stopped in front of Gregor. "We Balfins know how to guide the witches without them even knowing it."

Now Gregor looked confused. "How do we do that?"

"We train in their arts. We know their spells and their potions, and we are given tokens with their magic." From inside his robes, he withdrew a heavy medallion twice as large as Emenor's.

He twitched it side to side and muttered under his breath.

As the boys oohed, Gregor floated up out of his seat, waving his arms wildly.

"You think a witch is the only one who can learn to use magic?" Oakes whipped the medallion back under his robe, and Gregor dropped into his seat. "Never forget, young Gregor, the witches, though powerful, are few in number. The Balfin are many. Together, we are an unstoppable force."

"What good is an army when there isn't a war?" Hugo asked.

Oakes laughed. "My boy, the witches will never give up on their quest to rule Orkney. There is always a war in the works, this one just hasn't started yet. Class dismissed. Hugo, a word, please."

Hugo put his books into his bag. Was he about to get into trouble for missing morning classes?

But Oakes pointed at the drawing on his desk. "Where did you see a viken?"

"A viken?"

"Yes. Something the witches conjured up years ago. Created quite a stir. There was even rumor it killed one of their own before they destroyed it. How did you come to draw one?"

"Um, I'm not sure, I must have seen it in a book."

Oakes leaned in. "Because if there was a viken loose on this island, you would tell me, wouldn't you, Hugo?"

The professor's eyes were suddenly keen, staring into Hugo's.

Hugo nodded, crossing his fingers under the desk as he did.

# Chapter 7

Positively Potent Potions was Abigail's favorite class. Shelves crammed with crazily stacked jars—filled with oddities and ingredients for her famous potions—lined Madame Radisha's classroom. The musty room smelled like moldering mushrooms.

There were nineteen firstlings enrolled at the Tarkana Witch Academy. During their potions practice, they would each pair up with a partner. Endera always picked Nelly because she was smarter than Glorian.

The other girls each had their favorites—best friends that they matched off with—which usually left Abigail odd girl out unless a girl was absent. As Madame Radisha went on about the potent properties of powdered sneevil tusks, Abigail's thoughts drifted to her mother.

She hadn't thought about her in a long time. Abigail tried to imagine what she looked like. Had she ever come to visit her in the Creche? She wondered if they were alike at all.

Madame Radisha clapped her hands, snapping Abigail out of her daydreams.

"Now that we've learned how to brew our shreek-beetle potion, let's join partners."

Abigail groaned. She hadn't been paying attention at all and her Potions journal was blank.

She looked around, hoping some girl would take pity on her. Witchlings scurried by, but none of them even glanced at her. She caught Minxie's eye, but Glorian bellowed her name, and the girl shrugged at Abigail and moved on.

Abigail sighed. Alone it was. She would probably fail Potions and get kicked out in record time. They would send her back to the Creche to watch over the baby witchlings.

Someone tapped her shoulder.

"Looks like you need a partner."

Endera stood there with a fake smile so big it stretched her cheeks.

Abigail would rather fail Potions class than work with Endera, but before she could say anything, Madame Radisha cooed with joy.

"Endera, such a nice little witchling to partner with Abigail."

Abigail fumed as Endera beamed. One thing she knew for certain: Endera Tarkana didn't have a nice bone in her body.

"What are you up to?" Abigail whispered as Endera began opening jars on their table.

"Who, me? You heard ol' radish head. I'm just being nice." Endera smiled, but her eyes gleamed with spite.

Abigail sighed. She had no choice but to let Endera take the lead on making the potion since she didn't have a clue what to do.

"First, we need plenty of these." Endera picked up a jar with large black beetles crawling around and shook out several into the cauldron. "Next, we need a handful of shreeks' eyes. Grab that jar there." She pointed at a jar full of bulging eyeballs.

Abigail grimaced, then unscrewed the jar and dug her fingers into the slippery organs. Her stomach did a somersault. Witches weren't supposed to be affected by potion making, but sometimes she wanted to throw up. She quickly dropped them into the cauldron, then wiped her hands on her skirt.

"Now add the sneevil tusk powder," Endera said, nodding at a jar of white powder as she continued to stir the potion.

Abigail twisted the lid off. "How much should I add?"

Endera looked at her innocently. "Weren't you paying attention, Abigail?"

Abigail flushed. "Yes . . . I just . . . that is . . . I don't remember."

Endera rolled her eyes. "Fine, I'll tell you just this once. Madame Radisha said to dump the whole jar in."

Abigail hesitated. Was sneevil tusk powder potent? Why couldn't she remember anything? What kind of witch didn't know what sneevil tusk powder did?

*One who didn't pay attention in class.*

Endera drummed her fingers on the table. "Are you going to do anything? Or do I have to do all the work?"

Abigail sprinkled some powder in. The potion in the cauldron began to steam.

*Better not add too much.*

She started to tip the jar back, but Endera bumped her elbow, and the contents emptied into the pot.

"Oops." Endera grinned, taking a long step back.

Abigail didn't have time to move. The cauldron let out a high-pitched hissing noise and then blew up in her face, spraying beetle guts and shreek eyes everywhere.

The class fell silent as Madame Radisha rushed over.

"Abigail Tarkana, what in Odin's name were you thinking? Every witchling knows that sneevil tusk powder is too potent to use more than a teaspoon."

"I tried to tell her," Endera said innocently, "but she wouldn't listen."

Nelly slunk over, adding, "Yeah, I overheard her say Positively Potent Potions is a *duuuumb* class."

Madame Radisha pursed her lips and pointed a trembling finger at the door. "Out of my classroom. And don't come back until you've changed that attitude of yours. I have half a mind to fail you for the semester."

Tears stung Abigail's eyes.

She hated this school. She hated Endera. And she hated that everyone was staring at her, laughing. But it was just what Endera wanted, to see Abigail burst into tears.

She slowly pushed herself back from the table and stood up. Slimy trails of sneevil gook dripped from her hair. Beetle goo streaked her cheek.

Tucking her Potions journal into her book bag, she dipped her chin at Madame Radisha, spun on her heel, and walked out of the classroom.

# Chapter 8

Abigail swept her mop side to side, cleaning the sticky floor of Madame Radisha's classroom. She was going stir-crazy after three days of detention, doing endless chores after school and then locked in her room to study alone until supper.

"Are you trying to take my job?"

The cheerful voice came from a witchling who stood in the doorway. She held a mop in one hand and a bucket in the other. Slender, with pale skin and wide eyes, her dark hair was cut in a bob with bangs across her forehead.

"I have detention," Abigail said, pausing her mop. "Is that why you're here?"

"No. I work here." The girl set the bucket down and began mopping.

Abigail joined in. "I've seen you around. You're a secondling, aren't you?"

"Unofficially, yes. My name is Calla."

"I'm Abigail. What do you mean *unofficially?*" Abigail leaned on her mop to study the girl.

Calla kept mopping. "It means I'm a glitch-witch."

"Then you don't belong here," Abigail blurted out. She flushed, quickly adding, "I'm sorry. That was unkind."

Calla shrugged. "It's okay. I'm used to it. Madame Hestera is my great-aunt. She lets me clean her chambers and work around the school. In exchange, I'm allowed to attend classes."

"That must be hard," Abigail said. "To be unable to use magic."

Calla smiled, and her eyes sparkled. "That's okay. My magic will come in someday."

Abigail smiled back politely and wrung out her mop. She had never heard of a glitch-witch getting her magic. It seemed cruel to let Calla continue to learn spells and potions she would never be able to use.

"Would you like to hang out?" Calla asked. "I'm all done with my chores for the day. We could go to the Library and read spellbooks. There's a book on magical mushrooms—" She stopped at the look of hesitation on Abigail's face.

"It's not that I don't want to . . . " Abigail would love to have a friend inside the fortress walls, but today she had a plan to meet Hugo, detention or not.

Calla's sparkle dimmed. "Never mind. I'm sure you have better things to do."

She picked up her bucket and marched out of the room.

Abigail started to call her back to explain, then stopped when she heard the click-clack of shoes in the corridor signaling Madame Vex's arrival.

She followed Madame Vex up the dormitory stairs, quietly entering her room and waiting for the snick of the lock. As the sound of footsteps faded away, she went to her window and threw it open.

Her room was on the back side of the tower, high above the ground. She leaned out, feeling a bit dizzy at the height. Thick strands of ivy wrapped around the building. She tugged on a vine. It was tough, but was it strong enough to hold her?

She climbed out on the ledge, gripped a ropy length, then slowly lowered herself from the window. Her feet found toeholds in the leafy vines. She didn't dare look down. By the time the ground came into view, her arms ached. Puffing from exertion, she dropped the last few feet and brushed her hands off.

Time to find Hugo. She only hoped he hadn't given up on her.

Checking the courtyard was clear, she quickly crossed into the gardens. As she hurried down the path, movement caught her eye. There was someone pacing under a mulberry tree. Probably a witchling practicing her magic.

Abigail turned around to go a different way and then froze.

Endera was coming straight toward her.

# Chapter 9

ndera carefully combed her hair into place, tucking the long strands behind her ears. Smoothing her hands over her uniform, she made sure there were no wrinkles or marks. Satisfied her appearance was perfect, she skipped down the steps of the dormitory and went into the gardens.

Her mother had sent a note she wanted to see her, which meant it must be important. Melistra rarely bothered with her—which of course, Endera understood. A High Witch had many important duties. One day, Endera would take her place alongside her mother, and together they would knock that fusty Hestera off her perch as leader of their coven.

Heart thudding, Endera approached the tall figure that waited under a mulberry tree.

"Mother." Endera curtsied. "Did you hear I got high marks in Magical Maths?"

A flash of annoyance crossed Melistra's face. "I don't have time for your prattling. What have you done about getting rid of that witchling Abigail?"

Endera flushed. "I'm trying, Mother. She doesn't have her magic yet. She's going to fail Spectacular Spells any day."

Melistra grabbed her by the collar of her dress, twisting it painfully. "That's no excuse. I want her gone now."

Endera nodded, gasping out, "Yes, Mother."

Melistra let go, her stiff shoulders easing slightly. "I have something for you." She held out a thin leather tome. "My old spellbook. It will make your magic even stronger. I expect you to win High Witchling and make me proud."

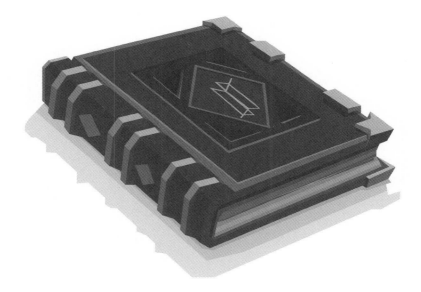

Endera took the book, staring at the old leather cover in awe. "Thank you. But isn't that cheating?"

"A witch does whatever it takes to succeed." Melistra turned to go.

Endera hesitated, then asked the question that had been bothering her. "Mother, may I ask, why is it . . . I mean . . . is Abigail so bad?"

Melistra froze and then turned slowly, her face white with rage. She raised her hand as if she were about to strike Endera. "Never challenge me again. Her mother was a traitor to the coven. That's all you need to know."

With a swish of her skirts, Melistra strode out of sight.

Endera watched her go, clutching the spellbook to her chest. She angrily swiped at the tear that escaped. She was a Tarkana witch, not some weepy girl. If her mother wanted Abigail gone, she would make the girl wish she had never been born.

# Chapter 10

Hugo waited in the branches of the jookberry tree. For the third day in a row, Abigail hadn't shown, which meant either she didn't want to see him anymore or something bad had happened.

What if she had been thrown into the dungeons for using her blue magic? Hugo swallowed back dread as he clutched the limb. He had heard stories about the rathos that lived down there, fiendish rodents the size of large housecats.

"Please, Abigail," he whispered. "Just give me a sign that you're okay."

"I'm right here, silly."

Hugo was so surprised to hear Abigail's voice he nearly fell out of the tree. He turned to find her standing on top of the wall behind him.

"How did you get up there?" he asked.

"I climbed a mulberry tree." She stepped onto the branch and carefully made her way over to Hugo, plopping down next to him. "I've been in detention all week, but I snuck out to meet you. As I was heading through the gardens, I nearly ran into Endera and her mother, Melistra."

"And?"

"I hid in the tree and listened in. Melistra gave Endera a spellbook and told her to get rid of me. And then she said my mother was a traitor." She shook her head, looking confused and frightened. "Why would she say that? And what am I going to do about it?"

Hugo squeezed her arm. "We need to get some answers. How long can you stay?"

"Supper's not for two hours."

"Perfect. I know just who to talk to."

Like every good scientist, Hugo had his sources—experts he could call on to answer questions. And the wisest person he knew was a sea captain named Jasper, who, if he was to be believed, was a Son of Aegir, the sea god who lived under the sea with the mermaids and mermen.

It was a quick walk from the Tarkana Fortress to the seaport of Jadewick. They slipped in among the sailors and Balfin soldiers who paraded along the docks. Hugo spied Jasper's ship at the end of the wharf. It listed to one side, as if it were slowly sinking. Ragged brown sails hung limply, looking as if a stiff wind would tear them to pieces.

The old sailor sat on the deck, sharpening a fishing knife on a stone. Long gray hair fell to his waist in a tangled mess. A length of rope belted up his weathered canvas pants. His skin was leathery brown, but his blue eyes were sharp as he looked them over.

"Who's your friend, lad?"

"Hello, Jasper, this is Abigail. May we come aboard?"

At his nod, they hopped onto the deck.

Hugo took his journal out. "What can you tell us about blue witchfire?"

The old sailor glanced around quickly. "Fool! You don't say things like that in public." He stood, bending on knobby knees to open a hatch. "Come below before you get us thrown into the Tarkana dungeons."

The cabin was small and cramped. A pair of bunks took up one end, leaving just enough space for a rickety table and two benches. Jasper sat down and lit a small oil lamp. The flickering glow cast long shadows on the walls.

"Tell me why you want to know," Jasper growled. His eyes looked a little wild in the light.

Hugo's heart hammered loudly in his ears. "Well, I . . . that is . . . we were just curious."

Jasper leaned forward, driving the tip of his knife into the table. "You're lying to me, boy. Do it again and I will drop your body at sea so only the fishies know where you end up."

"It was me," Abigail said quickly. "I used my magic to save Hugo from a sneevil in the swamp."

"And that awful beast," Hugo added.

"That's right. Each time my witchfire was—"

"Blue as the morning sky," Jasper breathed, his eyes glinting with excitement as he studied Abigail. "You must be Lissandra's child."

Abigail frowned. "Lissandra? No. My mother was Penelope. She died a long time ago."

"Who's Lissandra?" Hugo asked, writing her name down in his journal.

"She was a witch I knew." Jasper leaned on his elbows, studying her face. "And I'd stake my life you're her child."

Abigail bit her lip. "Old Nan's the one who told me her name was Penelope, but Madame Hestera had never heard of her. I overheard another witch say my mother was a traitor."

Jasper nodded. "Lissandra was running away with her babe when she died."

"Why? What happened?" Hugo asked.

The sailor rubbed his chin. "I'll tell you what I know, but I'll be needing a favor first. I'm looking for a creature about this high"—he put his hand to his waist—"covered in green fur. Talkative fella. You find him for me, and we'll talk."

Hugo nudged Abigail, and they got up and climbed the steps, but Jasper called after them.

"You mentioned a beast. What did it look like?"

Hugo turned. "Ugly as a Shun Kara but much bigger. It had beefy shoulders covered in a thick mane and teeth that looked like they could chew through granite. Professor Oakes called it a viken."

Jasper paled, putting a hand on the table to steady himself. "Stay out of the swamps, both of you. Whatever you do, don't go back in there."

# Chapter 11

Abigail hurried to her History of Witchery class. Witchlings were expected to be in their seats ready to recite the Witches' Code aloud when Madame Greef hobbled in on her walker. Any noise or fidgeting and the old witch would freeze, turning slowly to stare at the offending girl.

Then strange things would happen.

A whispering girl might find a frog suddenly leap out of her mouth. Or a squirming witchling might find a troop of fleas under her uniform to really give her something to fidget about.

But that's not why Abigail was hurrying.

Ever since Endera's mother had given her that spellbook, Endera had used spells from it to get Abigail into trouble.

The first day, Endera had cast her voice across the room, pitching it to sound exactly like Abigail's.

She had tasted frog in her throat all day.

The second day, Endera had made Abigail's seat hotter and hotter, until she finally shot to her feet with a yelp.

Madame Greef had not been pleased, which had earned Abigail an army of biting fleas under her uniform.

So today, Abigail planned to get to class early, so she could take a seat in the last row. If she was in the back, she could keep an eye on Endera and stay out of Madame Greef's sight.

Abigail rushed around the corner and ran straight into another witchling.

"Calla!"

"Hello, Abigail." The witchling's voice was cool as she leaned on her mop.

"Er, I haven't seen you around," Abigail said.

"I've been busy, you know, mopping floors and sitting in on classes, even though I don't belong here."

"Calla, I'm sorry, I didn't mean that."

The glitch-witch's face darkened with anger. "I saw you in town with that Balfin boy. You know why he's so nice to you? It's not because of your charm. He just wants your magic. That's right. That's all the Balfins want from witches, a token with magic. Just wait, he'll ask you for one. They all do."

The girl shoved past, leaving her mop and bucket behind. Abigail wanted to follow, make amends somehow, but there was no time. She ducked into the classroom and quickly scanned the rows. Endera sat in the center, an empty seat in front of her. With a wicked grin, she motioned Abigail to sit down.

No chance. There was still one seat in the far corner. She raced for it, elbowing another girl aside and sank down, sighing in relief.

Behind Endera, Glorian and Nelly burst into fits of laughter, elbowing each other as if they were in on some huge joke.

Uneasiness trickled down Abigail's spine. What was Endera up to now?

Madame Greef entered the room. The girls sat up straight in their chairs and began to recite the code.

> *"My witch's heart is made of stone*
> *Cold as winter, it cuts to the bone."*

The ancient hag shuffled her way forward, bent over her walker. Abigail tensed, waiting for something to go wrong. She stared at the back of Endera's head. The hateful witchling was sitting with her hands folded primly on her desk.

> *"My witch's soul is black as tar*
> *Forged in darkness to leave a scar."*

Abigail mouthed the words, but she began to sweat under her collar. There was a tension in the room, like an explosion about to happen.

> *"My witch's blood, it burns with power*
> *Cross me not or you will cower."*

Madame Greef was halfway to the front when Endera slipped her hand into her lap and lifted the old spellbook. With a sly look over her shoulder, Endera opened it and ran her fingers down a page, her lips moving silently.

A sudden charge of electricity made the hair on Abigail's arm stand up.

She tried to speak the words to the next verse, but her voice wouldn't work. She opened and closed her mouth, but nothing came out. A heaviness settled over her limbs, as if they weighed a ton. She stared at her hand, willing it to move, but was unable to lift it off the desk.

The door to the classroom quietly opened. Abigail had the power to turn her head, but that was all. The other girls went on reciting the code as if nothing at all were amiss.

*"My witch's hands will conjure evil*
*I plot and plan, I'm quite deceitful."*

Something hovered in the doorway. Abigail squinted, trying to see.

Was that Calla's mopping bucket?

It hovered in the air under its own power, then began to drift over the heads of the girls. No one blinked or even looked up as the bucket passed. Abigail lost sight of it, unable to tilt her chin back.

*"My witch's tongue will speak a curse*
*To bring you misery and so much worse."*

As the last verse finished, the room went quiet. A cold drop of water splashed on her head. And then another. And then, in a deluge of cold muckiness, the entire bucket spilled over her.

The class erupted into laughter as Abigail blinked away the liquid. Soapy grit stung her eyes. Strength returned to her limbs, and she shot to her feet, ready to give Endera a thrashing, but the door flew open, and Madame Vex swept in.

"What is the meaning of this ruckus?"

She gasped when she saw Abigail standing there dripping wet. The floating bucket dropped to the ground with a *bang*. Madame Vex marched over and held it up.

"Who is responsible for this?"

The room fell silent.

She held the bucket higher, marching up the aisle to the front of the class. "One of you cast a clever spell and dropped a bucket of water over Abigail's head. Stand up this instant—" she paused, and the pitch of her voice lowered to a purr "—so I can recognize that girl for being an outstanding witch."

There were shocked murmurs.

Surely, they were all going to be punished. Or made to do countless Magical Maths exercises.

But Madame Vex just smiled.

"My little witchlings, have you learned nothing in the weeks you've been here? This isn't the Balfin School for Ill-Mannered Boys. It's the Tarkana Academy for Witches. *Witches*," she added for emphasis as she prowled back and forth like a panther in front of them. "And witches are wonderfully wicked. So, I ask again, which delightful witchling used magic like this?"

Endera slowly raised her hand, but before she could speak, Minxie jumped to her feet.

"I did it," she said.

Madame Vex looked surprised. The entire class gasped.

"She's lying," Endera said, leaping to her feet. "I did it."

But it was too late. The rest of the girls had caught on. One by one, they jumped up, shouting they had done it, until the entire class was clamoring.

Even Abigail joined in, grinning as Endera's face grew redder and redder.

# Chapter 12

Hugo waited in the bushes behind the jookberry tree for Abigail to arrive. Today was the day he was going to ask her for a medallion. Surely, she would understand why he needed one once he explained. Gravel crunched on the path, and then Abigail came into view. Her pigtails were askew, and she smelled like musty wet wool.

"Abigail, finally!" he said, jumping out from behind the tree.

"Do you have news about my magic?" she snapped.

"No."

She frowned. "Then why are you here?"

"You're a crabby one," he said, stung by her sharp words.

"Sorry, it's just—"

"Endera?" he guessed.

"Yes." Abigail plopped down onto the ground. "She's using that spellbook to get me into trouble. Today, she cursed me with a freezing spell that took my voice away and left me unable to move a finger. Then she floated a bucket of dirty water over my head and dumped it on me. You know, I almost felt sorry for her after the way her mother spoke to her but not anymore."

Hugo clasped her hand. "If you gave me a medallion with magic, maybe I could help you."

Abigail gaped at the boy. "You want me to give you some of my magic? Is that why you're friends with me?" She pulled her hand back. "Because you want magic?"

"No!" He flushed. "It's not like that. I mean, I do want one. But that's not why I asked. Emenor's mad at me for taking his. I didn't want to ask you, but . . ."

She stared at him a long moment. "Fine. I'll see what I can do."

There was an awkward silence. Hugo wanted to apologize. But he shouldn't have to. It's not like he'd intended for any of this to happen, or that Emenor would have to destroy the medallion so Melistra wouldn't trace it back to him.

Before he could explain, the sound of voices reached them.

"It's Endera. Hide," Abigail said.

No sooner had they ducked into the nearby bushes than Endera and her two cronies came into view. Endera stopped, scanning the area, clutching her mother's spellbook.

"I want to go have a sweets," Glorian complained. "Cook was baking gally melon pudding."

"Quiet," Endera hissed. "Or I'll give you a taste of my magic. Abigail came this way. This time, I'm going to get rid of her for good." She patted the spellbook.

"What do you have against her?" Glorian asked. "We spend all our time going after her, but she's not that bad. She let me copy her answers in Magical Maths yesterday."

"Yeah, that's right," Nelly said. "She let me see her notes in Spectacular Spells. Why are you always on her?"

Endera grabbed the girl and pulled her close. "My mother wants her gone. Do you want to go ask her to explain why?"

Nelly shook her head.

"Then spread out. She's around here somewhere."

Nelly grumbled as she stalked down the path. Glorian slunk off to the right. Endera made a beeline for their hiding spot.

"She's headed this way," Hugo whispered.

"Move it," Abigail said, dragging him deeper into the shrubs.

They retreated farther into the garden, dodging among the brush. The paths were dense with foliage, and thorns pulled and tore at their clothes.

After several minutes, Hugo pulled up in a tiny clearing. "Do you think we lost them?"

The gardens were all quiet, save for the afternoon calls of birds. Abigail nodded, sighing with relief. "Yes, I think we're safe."

No sooner had she spoken than a splintering crack shattered the air. The ground dropped out from below their feet, and they were falling into space. Hugo flailed his arms, screaming loudly. Abigail screamed alongside him. They thwacked into the ground hard. Fortunately, they landed on a small pile of hay, or they surely would have shattered some bones.

Blurry sky peeked through a jagged hole in the roof. Hugo's glasses had come off. He sat up, feeling a bit woozy, and fumbled for them.

Abigail found them, wiping off the dirt, and put them back on his nose. "Are you okay?"

"No bones broken," he said, patting himself. "What is this place?"

Abigail stood, dusting off her dress. "It must be part of the dungeons. I think we fell through an old hay chute."

"Dungeons?" He gulped. "Have you heard about the rathos that live down here?" Panic made his voice rise. "I've heard they feast on the bones of the prisoners. They tunnel through stone to build their nests. They're eyes are like—"

Abigail cut him off. "I'm a Tarkana witch. Of course, I know about rathos. Quiet now, or you'll have them come running."

Hugo glared at her. "Why is it every time I'm with you, I end up in mortal danger?"

"It's your fault for climbing that jookberry tree in the first place," she pointed out.

A familiar face appeared in the opening over their heads.

"Endera, help!" Abigail called.

Next to Endera, Nelly and Glorian popped into view. The three witchlings looked shocked to see the two of them so far below them.

"Please," Hugo added. "There are rathos down here."

Endera's face drew into an evil smile. "Then they'll be well fed tonight. Enjoy your stay in the dungeons."

The girls pulled the broken boards over the opening until only a sliver of light shone through.

# Chapter 13

S team came out of Abigail's ears. The nerve of the girl, leaving them down here like that!

"When I get out of these dungeons, I'm going to settle things with Endera once and for all," she swore.

*Once* with a punch to her snotty nose, and *for all* with a kick to the shins.

"Never mind Endera," Hugo said. "We have to find a way out of here."

They looked around the chamber. There wasn't much besides stacks of empty wooden crates. A mound of old shields gathered dust in the corner.

A skittering sound made Hugo jump closer to her.

"What was that?" he asked.

"Probably a legion of rathos," she teased. "Any ideas how to escape?"

"We could stack those crates up and climb out," he said.

Abigail eyed the crates. "Good idea, but there aren't enough of them to get close to the ceiling, even if I stood on your shoulders. There must be a door." She shoved aside some of the crates and nearly cheered at the oval outline revealed. "See? Help me move these."

Hugo shoved, and Abigail pushed, and together they moved the crates away, revealing an ancient wooden door. It had an iron ring for a handle.

Hugo tugged on it. "It's stuck," he said.

Abigail grasped the handle, and Hugo braced one leg on the wall for leverage, but still it didn't budge.

Abigail studied it. "There're no hinges."

"So?"

"So . . . " She put her shoulder against it and pushed hard. With a pop, the door came unstuck, and she tumbled into the corridor.

Hugo slapped his forehead. "It opens outward. Good thinking, Abigail! You'd make a fine scientist."

But Abigail was hurriedly backing up. "Uh, Hugo, we have a problem."

"What?" Hugo peered around her and squeaked in horror.

The hallway was crawling with rathos. Their king-sized rodent bodies bristled with matted fur, eyes glittering hungrily in the dim light. The closest one bared pointy teeth, rising on its meaty back legs to hiss at them.

"Abigail, do something," Hugo said looking pasty gray.

"We have to get past," Abigail said. "I can try my witchfire, but there's a lot of them. I could use some help."

"Wait here."

Hugo ran into the storage room, returning with a

pair of rusty shields. "I'll scare them while you blast them. On the count of three. One, two . . ."

On three, Hugo began banging the metal discs together as Abigail released her crackling witchfire. It came easily now that she had mastered it, and she enjoyed the feel of the blue fire flowing from her fingertips.

The vermin quickly scattered, diving into cracks and crevices in the wall.

Hugo sagged with relief. "I really, really don't like those things. Let's get out of here."

They studied the dimly lit corridor. It was built out of stone blocks. Heavy wooden doors lined either side. Each had a small window inset with iron bars. Burned-out torches rested in notches every few feet. The air was cold and musty, as if no one had been down here in eons.

"Do you think anyone's inside these cells?" he whispered.

"Madame Vex said they haven't been used in centuries." Abigail hopped up and grabbed the bars at the first door, pulling her face to the opening. Scattered straw covered the ground. A set of rusted chains trailed from the wall ending in manacles.

"Empty," she said, jumping down.

They took turns checking every cell.

"Hugo, do you think Jasper's right? That my mother was this *Lissandra*?" Abigail asked.

"Maybe." Hugo jumped down as they walked to the next cell. "It would explain why Melistra said she was a traitor. Jasper said Lissandra was running away from the coven with her baby."

Abigail checked the next cell and then jumped down. "But why would she want to leave? A Tarkana witch has never left the coven."

Hugo shrugged. "How did she die?"

Abigail blinked. "I don't know. No one ever said, and I didn't think to ask."

They continued until they made it to the end of the hallway. There was only one cell left.

Abigail pulled herself up and peered inside. Besides the scattered hay, there was an old bucket and the bones of a long dead rathos. About to tell Hugo it was deserted, she squealed when a furry green creature moved out of the shadows and sat down on its haunches.

It was the oddest looking thing she had seen. It must have been double-jointed, because its knees went up to its ears, which were long and drooping, hanging down past its shoulders. Ignoring her, it started calmly chewing on its own toenail.

"There's something in there," Abigail whispered to Hugo.

"Talk to it. Find out who it is."

Abigail cleared her throat. "Hello there. Who are you?"

The creature paused its chewing to ask, "Who are yoooou?"

"I asked you first," she said.

"I asked you second, and two is greater than one," he answered snappily and went back to chewing on his toenail.

Frustrated, Abigail hopped down.

"Well?" Hugo asked.

"It's an annoying little pest. It spoke utter nonsense to me. You try."

Hugo dragged an old bucket over, and they both perched on it.

The creature was busily examining its toes one by one and then delicately nibbling them.

"HELLO!" Hugo shouted. "CAN YOU UNDERSTAND ME?"

The creature slowly lowered its leg, raising large almond-shaped eyes to look at them. "I assure you, child, my ears"—he flapped them—"are working quite perfectly."

Hugo looked at Abigail for guidance, and she gave him a nudge to go on.

"I'm Hugo, and this is Abigail."

The creature bowed its head. "I am Fetch. How kind of you to pay me a visit."

"He sounds intelligent," Abigail whispered to Hugo. "Ask him if he knows the way out."

"We're trapped down here, Mr. Fetch, sir. Do you know how we can get out?"

Fetch laughed, rolling from side to side on the floor as if it were the funniest thing he had ever heard. He finally stopped, sitting up to wipe tears from his eyes.

"Boy, if I knew that, I would have shaken this place days go. The food is *abooooominable*." He gave a visible shudder, and his furry green face turned a shade of purple.

"What did you do to end up here?" Hugo asked.

"My master, His Highest, sent me to look around."

"You're Odin's spy!" Abigail said, recalling Hestera's words.

"You're the one Jasper's looking for!" Hugo said at the same time.

Fetch lowered his head. "Indeed, you are both correct. I'm afraid Jasper is in for a long wait. Hestera has vowed to remove my head."

"Then we have to get you out of here," Abigail said.

Hugo turned to look at her. "Use your magic to open the door."

They jumped down. Hugo stepped to the side as Abigail shook out her hands and planted one foot. She took a deep breath. "*Fein kinter*," she whispered.

A familiar tingle ran down her arm as she flung her hands out. Blue fire sprang from her fingertips and blasted the hasp of the iron lock that hung on the door.

The lock grew red, and then the hasp burst open and tumbled to the ground.

Fetch crouched on the other side. "No time to waste. Let's make haste," he said, nimbly brushing past them and running up the steps on his spindly legs.

Abigail and Hugo quickly followed. At the top of the stairs, the corridor split into a forked path.

"Which way?" Hugo asked.

Fetch sniffed the air and pointed left. "This way."

They ran down the corridor, but as they came around a corner, muffled footsteps echoed ahead of them.

Fetch pulled them into the dark shadows of a small alcove carved into the rocks. They pressed themselves into the wall as the swish of skirts grew louder.

"This green pest will answer my questions or lose his head this very day!" Hestera's shrill voice demanded.

"Yes, madam." The deep male voice sounded like one of the Balfin guards. A sword rasped as he drew it out of its sheath.

The pair passed by without seeing them.

When the corridor was clear, they began to run. Behind them, a high-pitched scream of rage echoed as Hestera discovered her captive was gone.

They burst out of the dungeons into an outer corridor. Fortunately, no one was about, but Abigail was still in the middle of the Tarkana Fortress with a Balfin boy and a furry green creature to hide. She tried to think. They couldn't get to the gardens without crossing the wide-open courtyard in front of the classrooms.

"This way," she said, veering away toward the stables.

They snuck into the back door of the barn. A couple of Balfin groomsmen were hitching a pair of horses to a wagon piled with rotting kitchen garbage. Another flung a tarp over the pile to hold it in place.

"I've got an idea," Abigail whispered. "You two hide in the compost wagon, then jump out when it's outside the fortress. I have to get back to my room before Endera tells Madame Vex we were down there."

"You want us to climb in that?" Hugo asked, eyeing the smelly heap.

"Unless you have a better plan."

Hugo shook his head.

Fetch put one soft furry hand on her cheek. "Nice, indeed, Abigail Tarkana, to see you again."

"Again? But I've never met you before."

The funny little creature just nodded.

They waited until the other groomsman cleared out. Fetch and Hugo ran behind the wagon and climbed under the tarp.

Abigail sighed with relief. Now she had to hurry back to her room and hope she wasn't spotted. She slipped down the corridor, hugging the wall and keeping to the shadows. When she reached the dormitory, she hurried around back and quickly climbed the ivy hand over hand, tumbling into her room in an exhausted heap.

For once, not having any nosy roommates came in handy.

Quickly shrugging off her torn and dirty clothes, she

tied them in a bundle, and hid them under her mattress. Next, she put on a fresh uniform, brushed her hair, and braided it into neat pigtails. She sat down on the edge of her bed and opened her book on Potent Potions.

Her heart was beating fast, but she sat quietly. She turned the pages slowly, pretending to read, when the thundering sound of feet signaled visitors.

The door to her dormer flew open. Madame Vex stood in the doorway, eyes blazing. Endera and Nelly peered out from behind her. Glorian caught up, red-faced and puffing for air.

"Hello, Madame Vex," Abigail said sweetly. "Whatever is the matter?"

"You . . ." The headmistress looked confused to see Abigail sitting calmly on her bed. "I heard you were in the dungeons."

Abigail frowned. "The dungeons are off limits. I remember you telling us that on the first day. I'm sorry I went into the swamps last week. Endera was being so mean I just had to get away." A tear escaped down her cheek. "But I learned my lesson. I've been here in my room studying for Potions class all afternoon."

"Liar, I saw you!" Endera snarled.

Abigail blinked, keeping her face innocent. "I don't see how that's possible. Or perhaps it was you who was in the dungeons? Where were *you* all afternoon, Endera?"

Endera gawked at her.

"She's lying," Nelly said. "I saw her at the bottom of a hole. She fell in a secret entrance with that Balfin boy she's always hanging around."

"Yeah," Glorian added. "We can prove it."

"You mean prove you know where there's another entrance to the dungeons?" Abigail asked. "I'm sure

Madame Vex will want to know exactly where it is and what you were doing there. Unless, of course, you were just making it up to get me into trouble?" She smiled sweetly at Endera and then went back to reading her book.

"Well?" Madame Vex said, looking from her to Endera. "Is there a secret entrance or not?"

Endera opened her mouth and then closed it. Without another word, she shoved past Nelly and Glorian and left.

Abigail thought Madame Vex was going to pop a vessel. "Endera Tarkana, do not walk away from me! It will be detention for you every day for a month!"

She gave one last look at Abigail, then snorted her disgust and slammed the door.

# Chapter 14

The smell of rotting garbage made Hugo want to gag. Worse, he kept expecting an army of witches to descend on them and blast the carriage to bits. Fetch lay next to him, humming softly under his breath, as if he hadn't a care in the world.

The wagon stopped, and there was a loud rumbling as the gate rolled up. Then the wheels bumped forward, and they were outside the fortress. Relief made Hugo go limp. Behind them, bells clanged as an alarm was sounded, but the wagon kept going.

Hugo ticked off the minutes in his head until he was sure they were safely away from the Tarkana Fortress. He lifted one edge of the tarp, inhaling fresh air.

"Come on," he said. "We're near the edge of the woods. We can hide there until it's safe to go find Jasper."

Hugo waited for Fetch to jump first, then followed, tumbling in tall grass. The wagon rolled on. Suddenly, Fetch grabbed him by the collar and dragged him backward into the trees. The little green creature was much stronger than he looked.

Before Hugo could object to the rough handling, a pair of mounted soldiers thundered down the road and stopped the wagon.

The Balfin guardsmen yelled at the driver, who looked confused. They whipped off the tarp covering the pile of rotting kitchen scraps.

The two soldiers made retching noises as they poked the smelly heap with their swords, then replaced the tarp. The wagon driver threw his hands up and then cracked the whip over the horses and went on his way. The soldiers studied the trees, before climbing back onto their horses and heading back to the fortress.

"That was close," Hugo sighed. "Now I have to get you to Jasper, so he can get you far away from this place."

Fetch folded his arms. "I'm not leaving."

"But you can't stay here. If Hestera finds you, she'll—"

"I know what she'll do," he said calmly. "You will deliver a message to Jasper to take to my master, His Highest of High, Odin himself."

Reluctantly, Hugo pulled out his journal. "What's the message?"

"It is secret." Fetch held out one furry hand for the pad. He turned his back on Hugo and scrawled out a note. Then he folded it neatly into fours and held it out. "Triple swear, cross your heart, promise you won't read it?"

"I triple swear," Hugo said, crossing his heart three times. He tucked the note in his pocket. "Where will you go?"

"Oh, I'll be around. You might run into me now and again." Fetch saluted the boy and then scampered off into the trees, humming to himself.

Hugo trudged down the road into town. He made his way to the docks to Jasper's ship. He found the sailor in the same spot, sharpening his knife. Ducking under the rigging, he climbed on board.

Jasper silently shook his head when Hugo opened his mouth to tell him the news. Instead, the sailor led him down below, shutting the hatch before gripping the boy's arm.

"Well?"

"We found Fetch. We rescued him from the dungeon. Hestera was going to cut his head off."

"If that's true, then where is he?"

Hugo held out the note. "He said he was staying and for you to take this message to his master."

Jasper snatched the note, bringing it to his nose to smell it. "Did you read it, boy? I'll know if you're lying."

Hugo shook his head. "Fetch made me swear I wouldn't."

The sailor nodded, tucking the note away. "Then I best be off since my passenger isn't returning." He opened the hatch, but Hugo called after him.

"Wait. You promised to tell us about Abigail's magic if we helped you."

Jasper turned, letting the hatch close. "That I did. I suppose you've earned it. That blue witch is special."

"Is it because of her mother?"

The old sailor shook his head. "No. It was her father that changed her magic into something special."

Hugo frowned. "But Balfins don't have any magic of their own."

"Lissandra didn't consort with a black-hearted Balfin. She fell in love." He said the last part with a touch of disgust.

Now Hugo was sure Jasper was lying. "That's not possible. Witches don't love anything. It's written into their code. 'A witch's heart is made of stone,'" he quoted.

"Lissandra was different. She was always off wandering in the woods and gazing at the stars. I used to see her down here at the sea port, tossing petals into the water. That's how this all started. A sailor washed up on shore one day with no memory of where he'd come from. Lissandra found him and nursed him back to health."

Hugo wrote that down in his journal. "So her father was a sailor?"

Jasper held up a finger. "Not just any sailor. This one had powerful magic. I could smell it on him."

"What happened?"

Jasper's face closed up. "I've said enough for one day. A warning, boy. Abigail can't reveal her magic is blue, or the witches will know she's Lissandra's child. She'll be in grave danger, same as got her mother killed."

"But she'll get kicked out of the Tarkana Academy if she doesn't pass Spectacular Spells."

Jasper hesitated, then gave a short nod. "I reckon I can give her something for that. A reward for your help."

The sailor fished out a pendant from inside his tunic, lifted it over his head, and passed it to Hugo.

An ancient jade-green stone hung from a tarnished silver clasp.

"It's a sea emerald," Jasper explained. "A gift from my father, Aegir. If she calls on its magic, she can turn her witchfire green."

# Chapter 15

The best part of Endera and her two rotten friends having detention was that Abigail was free to meet Hugo in the gardens after school. When her last class ended, she skipped down the path to the jookberry tree, pigtails bouncing.

She peered up into the branches. No sign of Hugo. She sat down to wait, wrapping her arms around her knees.

"My, how you've grown."

Abigail started. A woman was sitting next to her on gracefully folded legs. Pale blonde hair fell down her back. Her gown was white, but it was her eyes that drew Abigail. They were a milky color that made her gasp.

The woman smiled. "Yes, I know I look quite strange. I am Vor, goddess of wisdom. And you are Abigail."

Abigail didn't know what to say. "That's right. What . . . what do you want with me?"

Vor smiled and lifted one hand. A white dove flew down from a tree and landed on it. She stroked it gently.

"You are like this dove, Abigail. Still bright with hope and goodness."

She blew on it softly, and the feathers began to change, fading from snowy white to gray, then darkening until it was black as night. Its body grew thicker and its beak longer until it had become a raven. It cawed harshly at Abigail.

"But the world can change you if you let the darkness in," Vor said. The goddess lifted her hand, and the raven flew off, wheeling into the sky with a chorus of angry caws. She turned her sightless eyes on Abigail. "You mustn't let the darkness win."

Abigail rested her chin on her knees for a long moment. Something about Vor's words rang true.

"Whenever I recite the Witches' Code, I feel it chipping away at me," she said quietly. "As if it's trying to remove the parts that feel things. I don't like it."

"Then fight it," Vor urged. "Don't become like the others of your kind."

Abigail's head came up. "How? If I want to be a great witch, I have to learn to be like them."

"You can be a great witch who is also merciful and kind. You can choose to be different *here*," she placed her palm lightly on Abigail's chest, "where it matters."

Abigail's heart ricocheted. "What if I don't want to be different?"

Vor withdrew her hand. "That is for you to decide." The woman rose nimbly. "Odin sent me to offer sanctuary to you—a chance to grow up away from this place. Or you can stay and let the darkness grow in you. I see both paths ahead. Neither is easy, and the hardest one of all is to fight against those that would make you into their pawn. Think it over carefully."

Vor's form shifted, and in her place a dozen white doves took to the sky, winging into the bright blue.

Abigail held her breath until the last dove disappeared

from sight, then blew it out in a long exhale. Leave the Tarkana coven? Fear sent cold shivers up her spine. She couldn't imagine life away from this place. As awful as it was at times, it was still her home.

Branches rustled overhead, and Hugo tumbled awkwardly onto the grass next to her.

"You're here!" he exclaimed. "I've been so worried about you. Was everything okay? Did Madame Vex punish you?"

Abigail turned, giving him a faint smile. "No, I turned the tables on Endera, and she ended up getting detention. They don't know how Fetch escaped, and no one's talking about it." She hesitated to tell him about the visit from Vor. It felt too private to share, even with Hugo.

"I have news about your magic," he burst out.

"Really?" Excitement kicked in her chest. "You know why it's blue?"

"Not exactly. Jasper's sure your mother was Lissandra, but he said you didn't get it from her."

"That can't be. It's not as if a Balfin could give me magic, silly."

"Your father wasn't a Balfin." He told her Jasper's story of the lost sailor.

"My father was a sailor? Where is he now? Does he know about me?" Her words tumbled out.

"Jasper wouldn't say, only that he had powerful magic. He said you can't let anyone know your magic is blue, or they'll know you're Lissandra's daughter, and you'll be in the same danger she was."

Abigail threw her hands up. "Then I'm finished."

"Not yet." He held out a silver chain with a large emerald dangling from it. "This can save you."

"It's beautiful," she whispered. "But what does it do?"

"It's a sea emerald. Jasper says if you wear it, you can use its magic to change the color of your witchfire to green."

Her eyes lit up. "Let's try it then."

She put the necklace on and put her hands up, drawing them in a circle, feeling the energy build. She thrust her palms forward, releasing it.

Sure enough, the witchfire that sputtered out was emerald, even brighter than Endera's.

"It works!" she shouted, jumping up and down with joy. "Now I can pass my Spectacular Spells exam!"

Hugo grinned. "There's something else. Fetch didn't leave."

"Why not?"

He shrugged. "He wouldn't say. He had me take a note to Jasper for his master, Odin."

"Why does a powerful god like Odin want to spy on the witches? We need to know what was in that note."

Hugo fidgeted, looking uncomfortable.

"What is it?"

The boy's face grew red. "Well, I triple promised Fetch I wouldn't read the note, and I didn't."

"But?" she prodded.

"But I didn't promise I wouldn't try to discover what he wrote." Hugo pulled out his notepad. He took his pencil and began lightly rubbing the edge of the lead back and forth across the page.

"What are you doing?" Abigail asked.

"You'll see."

Hugo's tongue stuck out between his teeth as he worked. A faint line appeared and then another.

When the paper was completely covered in shading, he held it up for Abigail to see. The pencil sketch had revealed words.

# THE DARK ONE RISES

"What do you suppose it means?"

"No idea. But we're making progress. We know your magic came from your dad. That's something."

"That's true. Thank you, Hugo." Abigail clasped the sea emerald, eyes dancing. "I'm off to find Madame Arisa and pass my Spectacular Spells exam. Wish me luck!"

# Chapter 16

Autumn had come and gone, dropping the temperature and leaving a layer of frost in the mornings. Life at the Tarkana Academy was much easier now that Abigail could use her magic. She was passing all her classes and had quickly risen to Madame Arisa's top student in Spectacular Spells. She and Hugo still met under the jookberry tree when they could, although they hadn't learned anything new about her magic.

With Yule Day fast approaching, Endera led the firstlings with the highest marks, closely followed by a witchling named Portia, the most beautiful firstling in their class. Abigail was catching up, but unless a miracle happened, she wouldn't have a chance at winning Head Witchling.

She followed a throng of girls into their Animals, Beasts, and Creatures class. Her ABCs instructor, Madame Barbosa, reminded Abigail of a cat. She could swear the teacher even had thin whiskers under her nose. And when she was happy with a student's work, she purred softly.

Abigail sat next to Minxie, ignoring Endera's glare. The girl still hadn't forgiven Abigail for getting her detention. Endera's anger put a small smile on Abigail's face as Madame Barbosa took her place at the front of the classroom.

"Today we will be learning how to charm a wild creature. There is a hierarchy of creatures the Tarkanas have created. The lowest is the rathos, then shreeks, sneevils, the Shun Kara, and of course, the mighty Omera."

She held up a drawing of an Omera. Wings spread wide, its sleek scaly body was black as night, and its pointed beak was lined with razor-sharp teeth. A spiked tail curved over its back, ready to strike a death blow.

"The mighty Omera cannot be tamed by any but the strongest of witches. They will as soon tear the flesh from your bones as allow you to ride them."

Abigail raised her hand. "Have you ever seen a viken?"

Madame Barbosa froze. Her mouth opened and closed. "Abigail Tarkana, why ever would you ask such a thing?"

Abigail shrugged. "I heard about one in a story."

"Vikens don't exist—at least, not anymore. Centuries ago, before the Tarkanas ran the coven, our ancestor Vena Volgrim created one. But it was deemed too vicious for even a Volgrim witch to handle, and the beast was put down."

Madame Barbosa dabbed at her forehead with a silk handkerchief, then pasted a smile back on her face.

"Enough talk of ancient beasts. Let us first conquer the simplest of creatures. Observe."

She whipped a black cloth off a cage. Inside, a hissing shreek gnawed at the bars, its wings unfurling. Red eyes glared at them as green spittle dripped from its open mouth.

"Never touch shreek spittle," she warned, putting on a pair of gloves. "It can burn like acid. Now, to tame this shreek, I must use my charm spell."

Madame Barbosa held up a hand, waving it in front of the winged rodent. "*Melly onus, stella kalira.*"

The shreek stopped hissing. Its red eyes glazed over, then turned black as its pupils dilated.

She opened the cage and lifted the creature out, setting it on the table. "Fetch me that chalk," she said, pointing.

The shreek dutifully flapped over to the board. It took the chalk in its beak and returned to drop it in her hand. She rubbed her knuckles over its head and then put it back in the cage.

Madame Barbosa unveiled another wild shreek. "Who would like to try?"

Hands shot up.

"Endera, why don't you have a go?"

Endera smugly got up and took a stance, holding her hands in front of her.

"*Melly onus, stella kalira.*"

The shreek kept on hissing and spitting at her.

"Try again, dear," Madame Barbosa said. "Louder this time."

"*Melly onus, stella kalira*!" she shouted.

The shreek stopped hissing, slowly folding its wings.

"Now open the door. Careful not to touch it."

Endera reached out and gingerly undid the latch. The shreek hopped onto the lip of the cage, waiting for instructions.

With a sly grin, Endera said, "Go fetch *her*." She swung around, pointing right at Abigail.

Abigail sat up straight, not sure she had heard correctly. Before she could hide, the shreek was circling her head, diving at her face, grabbing at her with its claws.

She screamed, batting at it and sending it flying across the room. The shreek careened into a large cage, knocking it off the table and breaking it open. A dozen shreeks flew out. Soon the room was filled with screeching shreeks and screaming girls.

Madame Vex barged into the room. "What is the meaning of this? This is the second time you've disturbed my Magical Maths class."

Her fist shot in the air, and a blast of crackling witch-fire shot out, sending the shreeks squealing for the safety of the cages.

She whirled around to glare at the class.

"What kind of firstling can't handle a simple shreek? I should send you all back to the Creche this instant."

Madame Barbosa swept forward. "There, there, Madame Vex, we're just learning our first charm spell. I'm sure they can do better."

"I'll expect them to prove that."

"What about a competition? To see who can bespell the most powerful creature?" Madame Barbosa purred.

"Yes, a competition," Madame Vex said. "We will send them out into the swamps to capture and tame a creature."

"The swamps?" Madame Barbosa's hand fluttered nervously. "Isn't that . . . dangerous for a firstling?"

Madame Vex snorted. "This unruly bunch seem able to handle anything. We can use the challenge to weed out the less capable ones."

"What kind of creature?" Portia asked.

Madame Barbosa spread her hands. "Anything that lives on this island. We will have a showing in, say, three days?" She looked at Madame Vex.

The headmistress nodded. "The remainder of your classes will be canceled until the competition is over. The witchling with the most powerful creature will earn enough credits to be declared Head Witchling for her class for the rest of the year."

The girls began whispering excitedly to each other, visions of the Head Witchling pin dancing in their eyes.

"But be warned," she held up one finger. "Failure to capture a creature will result in immediate expulsion."

That silenced the chatters.

A mixture of dread and excitement thrummed through Abigail as class was dismissed. Getting named Head Witchling was like being named the most popular girl in school. She had a vision of herself swanning into the Dining Hall wearing the gold pin and having all the girls clamor to sit with her.

All she had to do was go into the swamp and—a sudden wave of fear washed over her. Go into the swamp where the viken was? She shifted uneasily in her seat. She should warn Madame Barbosa about the beast. The girls would be out in the swamps alone. But if she said something, Madame Barbosa was sure to tell Madame Vex, which was bound to lead to more questions.

Her thoughts muddled, she left the classroom and ran smack into Calla in the hall.

"So, was I right?" The witchling's voice was cool.

"About what?"

"Did your little Balfin friend ask you for some magic?"

Abigail fumed. "So what if he did?"

"Then I proved my point. He only likes you for your magic." She turned and flounced off.

# Chapter 17

The nineteen firstlings had assembled in the gardens where Abigail usually met Hugo. Madame Barbosa was giving some of the girls final instructions before sending them into the swamps to find their creatures. Abigail was working up the courage to tell Madame Barbosa about the viken when Endera stepped in front of her.

"I'm going to win you know."

"Says who?" Abigail answered.

"Says me. You're too busy hanging around with that Balfin boy to be a proper witch. It's as if he's your best friend. Of course, he is your *only* friend."

The girls gathered around as they sensed a fight.

"He's not my friend at all," Abigail said hotly. "He's just an annoying boy who has no magic of his own and wants to steal mine."

"You're still going to lose," Endera said.

"Well, I intend to win," Abigail announced.

She had it all planned out. There were shreeks everywhere in the swamp. The winged rodents nested in every tree. She would find not one but two shreeks to bespell and train them to carry her bookbag for her.

Endera's eyes shone with spite. "Then let's place a wager on it."

"Have her be your servant for a month," Glorian suggested.

"Yeah, she can press your uniform and polish your boots," Nelly agreed.

But Endera waved them away. "If I win, you have to hand over that emerald necklace you never take off." She eyed the long silver chain around Abigail's neck.

Abigail clutched the emerald, tucking it into her dress for safekeeping. "No."

"No?" Endera arched one eyebrow. "Because you don't believe you can win?"

"No. It's just—"

"Face it, Abigail, you're going to lose, and you know it. Loser, loser," she taunted.

Abigail gave her a shove. "Am not."

Endera's face turned red, but she didn't push Abigail back. "Then take the bet."

"And what do I get if I win?" Abigail asked, all thoughts of warning Madame Barbosa having flown out of her head.

Endera gave a snarky little laugh. "You won't win, but for betting's sake, I'll . . ." She put a finger on her chin as she thought about it. "I know. I'll let you eat lunch with us for a month. Better than sitting by yourself every day."

Abigail burned with embarrassment. She was about to tell Endera to shove it when Calla pushed her aside.

"If she wins, she gets your spellbook," Calla said. "The one your mother gave you."

Abigail gasped along with the other girls. The spellbook was priceless. Endera wouldn't dare risk giving it up.

Endera looked pale, but she snapped back, "Mind your own business, glitch-witch. You shouldn't even be here."

Calla elbowed Abigail in the side, and something switched on in her.

"What's the matter? Afraid you're going to lose?" Abigail mocked. "Loser, loser."

There was dead silence. The witchlings all waited for Endera to find a way to make her take it back, but for once, the girl was stuck.

Endera's eyes narrowed into slivers of hate. "Fine. But you will never win, Abigail."

Madame Barbosa swept into the group, clapping her hands.

"Come, my little witchlings, gather around." Her cat eyes tilted upward, shimmering with excitement. "What a thrilling day to enter the swamps," she purred. "I cannot wait to see what you bring back, though I would stay away from those nasty sneevils. They never listen." She shook her head at some memory. "But, win or lose, you must present your creature here day after tomorrow or receive a failing grade in my class."

She snapped her fingers and the gate sprung open.

"Remember, if you run into any trouble, send up a blast of witchfire, and one of your instructors will assist you. Good luck to you all."

One by one they filed out and disappeared into the swamps. Abigail veered away from the other girls, determined to find her shreeks quickly so she could start training them. She was searching the branches for the tell-tale glowing eyes when a girl stepped out of the trees.

"Calla!" Abigail said in surprise. "What are you doing here?"

"You have to win, Abigail." Calla gripped Abigail's arm tight enough to hurt.

"I intend to. I'm searching for a pair of nice big shreeks."

"A pair of shreeks won't do. Endera's been taming a Shun Kara wolf for weeks now."

Disappointment flooded Abigail. No wonder the girl was so confident she was going to win.

"It's my problem, not yours," Abigail said, wrenching her arm free. "So just leave me to failing."

She plunged deeper into the swamps until the treetops were a dark canopy overhead. Trails of steam rose up from the marshy ground and her boots squished in the mud. When she was sure she was alone, Abigail leaned against the trunk of a blackened tree. Her hand went to the sea emerald. She lifted it from around her neck to study it. She couldn't bear to lose it. It would mean the end of her time at the Tarkana Academy.

The back of her neck prickled, as if there were eyes on her. Someone, or something, was watching her.

"Calla? Is that you?" she called, looking around.

The swamps had gone quiet. The shreeks that hung in the trees weren't squealing. Even the noisy insects had stopped their buzzing. A deep chuffing sound reached her. As if something large was breathing in and out. Something very close.

Right behind her, in fact.

Abigail slowly turned. Her heart beat wildly as she made out the outline of a hulking shadow lurking in the bushes. She took a careful step backward. If she was quiet, she might be able to get away. She took another step and felt a stick bend under her boot. She tried to stop herself but couldn't freeze in time. The stick cracked loudly as it snapped in half.

With a snarling roar, the viken pounced in front of her.

"*Melly onus, stella kalira*," Abigail shouted, hoping to charm it into submission.

It just roared louder. Fetid breath washed over her as it stalked closer. A line of drool hung from its jaw.

She sent a blast of witchfire at the viken. The first one hit it square in the chest, and the beast yelped, jumping backward. She fired again and again as it circled her, trying to find a way in.

Her arm quickly grew tired. Magic like this was draining. The viken stayed just out of range, toying with her as her witchfire began to sputter.

A dark shadow blocked out the sun as a high-pitched screech filled the air. Abigail looked up in shock. Winging down on them was a frightening creature, its smooth scales black as pitch. The spike at the end of its long tail could impale her with a single strike. Gleaming teeth protruded from its beak. Her breath caught as she recognized it from Madame Barbosa's picture.

An Omera.

*How could things have gotten worse?*

She closed her eyes as it opened its jaws, sure it was about to rip her head off.

Sharp talons bit into her shoulders and swept her into the air. It lifted her above the murky swamp and out of the reach of the viken's snapping jaws.

# Chapter 18

Hugo sat in the jookberry tree long after the witchlings had stampeded into the swamps. Abigail's
words had cut deep.

*He's not my friend at all, just an annoying Balfin boy
who wants to steal my magic.*

Was that really what she thought of him?

She had to know he wasn't her friend just to get magic.
He rubbed the bruise on his arm, the one Emenor had left
that morning. His brother was getting impatient. Still, Hugo
would take a beating rather than lose Abigail's friendship.

He climbed down from the tree and followed the witchlings, keeping a safe distance. He ducked behind a trunk as
he came across the stout one, Glorian. She was trying to
coax a fledgling shreek from its nest into a small cage. The
shreek cried pitifully for its mother, then nipped Glorian's
finger, making her yelp. The witchling gave up, stomping
off to find another creature.

But where was Abigail?

Pairs of tracks headed off in every direction. Knowing
Abigail, she would stay as far away from the other witch-

lings as possible. He spied a single pair of tracks that led deeper into the swamps.

He followed them, keeping close to the tree trunks to hide from the girls that trickled through. After several minutes of walking, the swamp grew eerily quiet, with only the occasional cries of shreeks.

Hugo had never been this deep in the swamp. It was nearly dark; the dead branches gnarled and twisted together so tightly overhead hardly any light was let in.

He cleared his throat, about to call for Abigail, when he heard her scream.

"Abigail! I'm coming," he shouted, breaking into a run. But when he got to the spot, it was empty. "Abigail? Where are you?" he called. Clawed footprints marred the muddy ground. Something glinted. He knelt down and dug into the damp earth.

Jasper's sea emerald. She must have dropped it when she was attacked.

"She's not here," a raspy voice called.

Hugo whirled around. "Jasper! You're back!"

"Aye. We've been tracking that viken. You shouldn't be out here alone."

Behind him, Fetch appeared, wringing his green paws.

"Come, no time for time to pass," Fetch said, beckoning at them. "We must rescue the blue witch before it's too late."

The little creature turned and scampered into the woods.

"You coming, lad?" Jasper looked down at him with steely blue eyes.

"Where are we going?" Hugo asked. "I have to be home in time for supper."

The sailor put a hand on Hugo's shoulder.

"Where we're going, there's no supper waiting. There's only treacherous swamps, quicksand bogs, and wild sneevils. I won't blame you if you turn around and go home. You're naught but a school boy."

Hugo's heart quaked in his chest. He wanted to go home. Have his mother's fig pudding. Sleep in his own bed. Even have his brother Emenor pound on him for using his medallion.

But instead he nodded at Jasper.

"I'm in."

Because Hugo wasn't about to give up on Abigail, even if Abigail had given up on him.

# Chapter 19

Abigail kept her eyes closed as the wind rushed past her face. The Omera's claws dug into her shoulders but only tight enough to grip her.

"Put me down," she shouted for the hundredth time, beating on its scaly legs. She'd escaped one monster only to be taken by another.

It kept flapping its wings, ignoring her pleas.

She looked around trying to see where they were headed, but a layer of fog covered the swamps. As they flew on, the fog turned to mist and Abigail could make out the rise of a distant peak. This was the eastern end of Balfour Island, a wild untamed place filled with roaming Shun Kara wolves, packs of sneevils, and other ghastly creatures.

The Omera flew steadily until it reached the peak, then flew straight up a sheer cliff until it reached a stone ledge. It released her, sending her tumbling, and landed next to her with a rasp of its claws.

Abigail scuffed her knees on the rough stone, but no bones were broken. Standing on shaky legs, she looked around, nearly fainting at how high up they were.

The Omera snorted at her, blowing steam from its nostrils.

"What do you want?" she said, stinging and aching. "Why did you bring me here?"

The Omera jerked its head toward a tall pile of sticks. Not a pile. A nest.

"You want me to look inside?" Abigail asked and then drew back as a horrible thought occurred. "Or am I the next meal for your hatchlings?"

The creature snorted again and then whimpered softly.

Abigail sighed. "Fine. I suppose if you wanted to eat me, you would have already." She stalked over to the nest. The tangle of sticks and moss was taller than she was. Taking a step up onto the twisted branches, she peered over the top.

Inside were two inky black hatchlings, fresh out of their shells, gaping at her with wide open maws. Their baby teeth were already sharp. But a third one hadn't hatched yet.

She looked down at the Omera. "What is it you want me to do?"

The Omera leapt inside the nest, nudging the unhatched egg toward Abigail, then waited.

It was crazy, but the Omera seemed to want her to do something about her unhatched egg. Abigail warily climbed onto the lip of the nest, legs dangling. The two hatchlings tried to nip at her ankles, but the mama Omera growled at them, and they yelped, retreating behind her.

Abigail slowly lowered herself into the nest. Stretching her hand out, she touched the unhatched egg. The shell was surprisingly warm to the touch. She knelt closer and put her ear to the speckled surface, listening.

*Whompa, whomp*

*Whompa, whomp*

Startled, she looked up at the Omera. "Your baby is still alive."

The Omera's eyes looked watery, as if it was tearing up.

"You're just a big softy, aren't you," Abigail said. "Why isn't your baby hatching?"

The Omera settled down and put its scaly head on its claws, staring longingly at the egg.

"You don't know," Abigail guessed. "And you're worried." She paced around the egg, studying it from every angle. "But why drag me into it?"

One of the hatchlings decided Abigail was too tasty a treat to resist and darted out from behind its mother, trying to chomp down on her leg. Instinctively, Abigail zapped it with a dazzling blast of blue witchfire. It shocked the baby Omera but didn't hurt it.

The mother Omera didn't hesitate to swing her spiked tail, sending the hatchling spinning out of the nest to land with a wailing *thud* on the stone ledge.

The mama Omera jerked her head at the egg and then back at Abigail's hands.

Abigail looked down at them. "You want me to use my witchfire on the egg? That's why you took me? But what if I hurt it?"

The Omera moaned, a long deep sound.

Even Abigail understood that. "If I don't do something, it will die anyway."

The Omera chuffed. It waited, talons clenched around the sticks. Behind it, the other hatchling peered out with curious eyes.

Abigail went back to the egg, putting her hands on it again.

*Whompa, whomp*

She shook her head. "I'm not sure I can help. I'm sorry."

The Omera growled low, and Abigail looked into its eyes, reading the message clearly.

It was up to her to get the hatchling out, or she wasn't leaving this nest.

# Chapter 20

Hugo's boot sank deep into the oozing mud. He was so tired he could barely pull his foot loose. Insects bit at his neck, leaving stinging welts. Jasper and Fetch marched headlong into the swamps without missing a step.

"Keep up, lad," Jasper tossed over his shoulder. "And watch out for quicksand bogs. You don't want to get swallowed up."

Hugo sighed, shoulders slumping, then yanked his boot free and tried to pick up his pace.

The previous night they had made camp on a grassy knoll surrounded by dark murky water. Slithering animals and shrieking night birds had made it nearly impossible for Hugo to fall asleep. He was sure a pack of sneevils was going to overrun their camp at any time. And then something had crawled under his shirt, making him scream in fear.

Jasper had pounced on him, clamping a hand over his mouth and warning him the next scream might be his last.

After that, Hugo hadn't slept a wink.

Which was why his eyes now felt like sandpaper, and he could barely take another step.

He wondered if his parents were worried about him or if they figured he was just off on his scientific adventures. He'd spent the night in the woods before, but he always told them where he was going.

He tried lifting his boot, only this time it wouldn't budge. He tugged on the leather, trying to free it from the heavy mud.

"Hold up," he called, pulling harder. His foot slipped out of the boot, and he fell backward on his bottom in the mud. Cold water seeped through his clothes, soaking him to the skin. Worse, when he looked up, the sailor and the green pest were nowhere in sight.

Great. They had left him. Frustrated tears burned his eyes.

Hugo used both hands to wrench his boot out of the muck. It released with a loud squelch, flinging mud in his face and spattering his glasses. He shoved his foot in the boot, ignoring the cold mud that squished between his toes, and took his glasses off, wiping them clean with his sleeve.

A blurry figure moved into sight. Jasper must have come back for him.

"Over here," he called, putting his glasses on.

Then he wished he hadn't. Because it wasn't Jasper standing there.

The viken's head hung down, one paw clawing at the thick mud.

"Easy," Hugo said, taking a step back. "You don't want to eat me. I'm skin and bones."

The viken advanced, glowering. It snarled, snapping at the air.

"I probably taste terrible," Hugo rambled on, "like the world's worst mutton."

At the mention of mutton, the viken's pink tongue lolled out of its mouth, and a strand of drool dribbled out.

Hugo tried to think. He was a scientist, solving problems was his strength.

Problem: the viken was about to kill him.

Solution: stop the viken before it could get to him.

But how? He had no weapon. No way to fight this beast.

He took a trembling step backward and nearly lost his balance. His left foot sank up to his knee before he fell forward onto his hands. He turned his head, looking closely at the ground. Jasper had warned him about quicksand bogs. This one looked about four feet wide. The mud was yellowish and smooth on top.

Hugo took a healthy step to the side, moving slowly around the bog until it was between him and the hairy beast. Reaching out, he grabbed a big stick.

The viken prowled closer, eyes locked on Hugo.

"Please don't eat me," Hugo begged, not having to feign his terror. "I'm just a helpless boy."

Knees shaking, he lowered himself to kneel at the edge of the quicksand, making himself an easy target. The viken fairly grinned as its jaws widened in anticipation. Hugo closed his eyes as the beast leaped, landing dead center in the bog, spraying him with yellow mud.

When he opened his eyes, the viken had sunk up to its shoulders. It pawed furiously at the surface, clawing its way to the side, howling in shock. Hugo scrambled up, using the stick to shove on its chest, pushing it back in.

The beast snarled, clamping its powerful jaws down on the flimsy limb, snapping it in half, but the weight of the quicksand held it, and the viken began to sink. First its shoulders disappeared, then its head, and last, the tip of its snout. With a loud belch of air, the bog swallowed it whole.

Hugo sank down in relief as Jasper burst out of the trees. "I heard the howling. What is it, lad?"

"The viken—it came after me. But I tricked it into jumping into the bog," he said, his teeth chattering with fear.

Jasper put his hand out, hauling Hugo to his feet.

"Good work, lad. But there's no time to waste. We found the blue witch."

# Chapter 21

After a night shivering in one corner of the nest, Abigail woke up tired and hungry. She had hurled magic at the obstinate egg over and over, but no matter how hard she'd tried, her magic hadn't made the tiniest crack in the speckled shell.

She wished Hugo was here. He would pull out his trusty journal and come up with a solution for cracking this egg open, because she certainly didn't have one.

Feeling thirsty, Abigail climbed out of the nest and wandered over to the stream that trickled down the back wall of the aerie. She cupped her hand and drank deeply, then splashed her face, washing the grime away. Her braids had come undone and she had lost one of the ties, so she settled for tying her hair back in a ponytail.

Out of the corner of her eye, she caught Big Mama, the mother Omera, studying her. The two hatchlings were napping. Abigail had named the nasty one that kept nipping at her ankles Vexer, after her headmistress, and the nice one she dubbed Waxer.

She turned her face to the sun, letting the rays bathe her. She needed something to make her magic stronger. Something to amplify it. But what?

If only she had Jasper's sea emerald, it might help.

Waxer waddled over on gangly legs and butted its head up next to her. She scratched its scaly black nose.

"Any ideas?" she asked. It looked up at her with ebony eyes and chuffed softly. She sighed. "Yeah, me neither."

She folded her arms and leaned against the stone. She started daydreaming, imagining she was sitting under the jookberry tree, laughing with Hugo.

"Abigail."

She smiled, keeping her eyes closed.  Now she really was imagining things. It had sounded as if Hugo were calling her name. Maybe hunger was making her hallucinate.

"Abigail!"

Her eyes flew open. She hadn't imagined that. It was Hugo's voice— faint but definitely close by.

She ran to the ledge and looked over. She almost fainted. Climbing the cliff face was an unlikely trio led by Jasper, who was pulling himself up with wiry arms. Behind him, the little scamp Fetch hopped rock to rock. Then came Hugo.

He waved at her.

She wanted to wave back, but instead she shouted, cupping her hands so her voice would carry. "Are you crazy? What if you fall?"

But she grinned so wide her face hurt.

He had come for her. For some reason, that made her want to sing.

Big Mama wasn't so happy to have visitors. She launched herself off the ledge and soared in a circle, then folded her wings and dive-bombed the intruders.

Abigail screamed a warning, but Hugo held up something shiny in his hand.

It was the sea emerald. The sunlight caught it just right and it sent out a blaze of green light that blinded Big Mama. The Omera reared back, flapping her wings, and spun away to make another circle.

"Hurry!" Abigail called. "Before she comes back."

Vexer took advantage of Abigail's distraction and nipped her on the calf. She whirled, sending out a blast of witchfire strong enough to make the hatchling yelp.

"Do that again and I'll sizzle your tail off!"

Wisely, it went running behind the nest.

Waxer waddled up beside her, bleating encouragement. The trio of rescuers were close. Jasper's elbow landed on the ledge. Abigail grasped his shoulders and helped him over.

Then came Fetch. The creature nimbly flipped himself up, landing on two feet.

Abigail went back for Hugo, but the boy had frozen in place, out of reach. She lifted her head and saw the reason.

Another Omera was coming straight for him. It was a different one, even larger, with brawny shoulders. Jagged teeth glinted in the sunlight. Abigail couldn't be sure, but she had a feeling this was Big Daddy.

Its wings pounded, and it roared as it stretched its head out, jaws open, ready to devour Hugo in one snap.

"Noooo!"

Abigail planted her feet and thrust her palms forward, determined to save her friend. A steady stream of blue fire shot out. Though her magic was growing stronger, the sizzle didn't even dent the Omera's thick hide. The flying beast kept coming.

Jasper leaned out over the ledge. "Quick, boy, give me your hand!"

Hugo snapped out of it, scrambling higher to reach Jasper's outstretched hand. The sailor pulled him up with one mighty heave.

They huddled on the ledge as the monstrous Omera bore down on them. There was nowhere to hide, nowhere to run.

They were as good as dead.

And then Waxer waddled in front of them and flared its frail wings, opening its mouth to squawk at its daddy.

The big Omera's eyes widened in shock. It tried to pull up, but it was coming too fast. It veered over their heads and crashed into the back wall, slumping to the ground with a loud *oomph*.

"You saved us, Waxer!" Abigail gave the baby Omera a hug.

"Don't I get a hug?"

Hugo's face was red and sweaty. His school uniform was in shreds. He had mud everywhere. A scratch marred his cheek, and his glasses were on crooked. He was a sorry mess, but Abigail had never been so happy to see another person in her whole life.

She flung her arms around him and squeezed him tight. "I can't believe you came to rescue me."

"Of course, I came. You're my best friend." His eyes slid away from hers. "Er, I heard what you said. To the other girls."

"You heard that?" She groaned. "I'm sorry I was such a jerk."

"That's all right, as long as . . . that is . . . You didn't mean it, did you?" He gave her a hopeful look.

She punched his arm. "Don't be a dope, silly."

Jasper put his hand on her shoulder. "You're all right, lass? They haven't harmed you?"

She shook her head. "Big Mama wants me to help hatch one of her eggs, but so far my magic hasn't been able to even scratch it."

"Well, we'd better think of something quick before that giant Omera wakes up," Hugo said. "I don't think he'll be very forgiving."

Big Mama thudded down on the ledge, eyeing the strangers warily as she called to her babies. Waxer left Abigail, looking sadly over its shoulder, and waddled over. The protective Omera shooed her babies behind her.

But where was Fetch?

The unhatched Omera egg, speckled blue and the size of a small boulder, appeared at the top of the nest. Behind it, Abigail could see Fetch pushing with his scrawny arms. The egg teetered, then dropped, hitting the stone ledge. It bounced twice, rolling dangerously close to the edge.

Big Mama panicked, rushing forward, but Hugo dove and grabbed it with both hands, stopping the precious egg before it fell.

There were several sighs of relief.

The Omera nudged her egg to the center of the ledge and then settled down beside it. Her eyes were more worried than ever.

Abigail put her hands on the shell. It was still warm but . . . She placed her ear to the shell, listening.

*Whompa . . .*

*Whompa . . .*

The heartbeat was slowing down.

She looked up at the sailor. "Please, we have to do something."

Jasper rubbed his chin. "You say your magic won't open it?"

She shook her head. "I've tried throwing witchfire at it over and over."

Jasper scowled. "That's not your only magic, child. You need to dig deeper. Find your true magic. The magic of your father."

"What are you talking about?" Abigail asked.

Jasper took a deep breath. "Long ago, the mighty Thor was traveling in the icy north with a companion, a giant named Aurvandil the Brave. Thor carried him in a basket on his back. One of Aurvandil's toes stuck out and froze. Thor broke off the toe and threw it into the sky, and it became the star we call Rigel."

Abigail's head swirled with confusion. "What does that have to do with my magic?"

"Rigel was the name of the sailor who washed up to shore. Abigail, I believe your father *is* the morning star. The proof is in your witchfire. It burns the same cerulean blue as the star."

"But how is that possible?" Hugo asked.

"With the gods, all things are possible," Fetch pronounced, one finger in the air, then he took Abigail's hand in his soft paw, "if you but believe."

"I used to see your mother walking the shoreline, her eyes on the stars," Jasper added. "I don't know if it was her magic that did it or his, but whatever it was, Rigel descended and left you with a powerful gift."

Big Daddy moaned and began to stir.

"Abigail, it's now or never," Hugo said.

"Okay, don't rush me." She ran her hands over the egg one more time.

"Don't think about it," Jasper urged. "Your father's magic is in there. Open the door that's blocking it."

Abigail cleared her throat, dug the toes of her boot into the stone, and tried to think of her magic, but her mind was blank. She couldn't even draw up a trickle of witchfire, let alone find a cure for this stubborn hatchling.

Frustration rose in her. She was going to fail, and they were all going to die here on this ledge.

# Chapter 22

And then Hugo was there at her side. "Close your eyes and imagine the door that's blocking your magic."

"What good will that do?" she answered crossly.

"My dad taught me to do this when I have a problem I can't solve. If I can imagine it, I can see my way past it."

She grumbled but closed her eyes tightly. It took a moment, and then . . . there it was. A door floated into view. It was red—tall and imposing with a brass knocker.

"Got it," she said. She reached out her hand and tried the knob. "It's locked."

"Now imagine a key that can open it."

Keeping her eyes screwed shut, she pictured a key, a large silver skeleton one like Madame Vex used to lock her in her room.

A key materialized in front of her. Hugo's trick was working! She plucked it out of the air.

"Okay, I have it."

"Put the key in the lock."

Abigail stuck the key into the keyhole. She twisted it to the right, but nothing happened. She tried again, twisting to the left, and the lock clicked.

"Its opening," she said with an excited gasp.

"Then go inside," Hugo urged.

Abigail slowly pushed the door open and blinked.

Inside, the light was so blinding she couldn't make anything out.

"It's too bright. I can't see anything," she said, panicking. "I have to go back."

"No," Hugo said firmly. "Go forward. I'll be right there with you. Just imagine me next to you."

Abigail concentrated, closing her eyes tighter, and held out her hand. Hugo's warm hand grasped hers. When she turned her head, he was standing next to her in the bright room.

"Do you see it?" she asked.

"Yes." He sounded awestruck. "It's like we're really here. Whatever you're doing, it's working."

"Where do we go?" She squinted to see in the blinding light.

"There," he pointed. On the far wall was just the faintest outline of another door.

He began dragging her forward, but she hesitated.

"No." She dug her heels in. "I can't go in there."

"We have to, Abigail."

"No!" She yanked her arm free. "You don't know anything, Hugo Suppermill. You're just a Balfin boy with no magic."

He sighed. "Which you keep reminding me of. But I'm also your friend. Why are you so afraid?"

It took Abigail a moment before she could speak. "He's in there," she whispered, lowering her eyes.

"Who is?"

"My father."

Hugo was silent a moment, then he said, "It will be okay, Abigail. I'll be right here."

"Promise you won't leave my side?"

"Promise."

He squeezed her hand, and they began walking across the floor. The light bounced off them, dancing on their skin. Abigail held her hand up, and the light shone around it.

They reached the door. There was no handle, no lock. The surface was warm to the touch. She pushed it open and stared in wonder.

"Where are we?" Hugo asked.

They were standing on the same bluff, but there was no nest, no Omeras, no Jasper or Fetch. It was the same place but a different time. Overhead, stars blazed in a spangled blanket of lights.

"I'm not sure." Warm air trailed across her skin. She hesitated, and then she whispered, "Father . . . are you here?"

The breeze stirred, ruffling her hair.

A star in the sky burned brighter, so bright it was actually blue, pulsing with light.

Encouraged, she raised her voice. "Please, Father, I need to tap into my magic. The magic you gave me. Can you help me?"

A soft lilting melody began to play. A pang ran through her. Abigail had heard that song before, a long time ago. She hummed along. The music grew louder, as if pleased by her response.

The blue star glowed brighter and brighter until, suddenly, it shot through the night sky, heading straight for them.

They ducked as it hit the stone ledge in an explosion of light.

Abigail put a hand up to shield her eyes as Hugo squinted next to her. After a moment, the light dimmed enough for them to see the outline of a man.

He was slender and tall, with blond hair, fair skin, and broad shoulders. He wore a simple shirt, tucked into breeches, and black boots.

"Father?"

He walked toward her. His eyes were as blue as the star, shimmering with curiosity and power.

He stopped in front of her, kneeling so their faces were even.

"Hello, little one."

"Is it . . . is it really you?"

He swept her into his arms, holding her tight. "I never thought I would hold you like this," he said softly.

Abigail trembled as she was wrapped in his warmth. It was the strangest feeling in the world. Warm, crinkly, filling every pore with love. She had never been held like this in her life. Cuddling wasn't done at the Creche.

Then a memory returned.

Her mother had held her like this once, wrapped in

a warm blanket close to her chest. A tear slid down her cheek as her father filled her with a lifetime of love.

"Who are you? Where did you come from? How did you meet my mother?" She tripped over the words as the questions poured out.

"I have no memory of who I once was," he said. "I shone down from the sky, seeing and watching but having no form. Until I saw her."

"Who?" Hugo asked.

"Lissandra." He said her name as if it were a caress. "She called to me every night, wishing, pleading for something of her own to love."

"Witches don't love anything," Abigail said, feeling a tear in her heart as she did because it was a lie. Abigail loved a good many things. But for how long? How long before the witches stamped it out of her?

Rigel smiled at a memory. "This one did. Her wish must have been powerful because I found myself awake in a strange body, floating in the sea. I washed up on shore, and there she was. I was given one week with her before I had to return."

He released Abigail, taking a step back, and she knew their time was at an end. He was already beginning to fade, his shape sparkling with a strange energy.

She flung her hands out, reaching for him. "Don't go. Please, I need your help. I need you to guide me. I'm afraid."

He took her hands in his, enveloping them in warmth as blue light swirled around him. She squinted as his eyes burned so bright they could have been a thousand suns. His skin lit up with a vibrant glow that ran from his hands to hers, up her arms, sending ripples throughout her body. Energy hummed through her, filling her veins with so much power she thought she might burst.

"Trust your heart, child. That is the only guide you need."

Rigel released her hands, tilting his head back to look upward. Light shot out of every pore in his body, growing brighter until in a burst of radiant light, he vanished.

Abigail fainted.

When she opened her eyes, she was lying on her back on the stone ledge. Hugo and Jasper leaned over her, looking worried.

"Are you okay?" Hugo asked as Jasper helped her to her feet, steadying her as she swayed.

"Yes." She felt fine, better than fine, like she could leap over the sun in one jump. "Did I really just meet my father?"

"I think so. I'm not really sure what happened," Hugo said.

"One second you were there, and then you joined hands and you both vanished," Jasper said.

Fetch took Abigail's hand, rubbing it between his furred paws, then put it to his face. "You are filled with starshine, Abigail. Use it to crack the egg so that we might depart."

Abigail lined up with the egg again. The daddy Omera was stirring, groaning and twitching his limbs. Big Mama rose up, her eyes glowing with excitement. The two baby Omeras peeked out from behind her.

"Okay, here goes nothing," Abigail said. She waved her hands in a tight circle, murmuring to herself. She usually said *fein kinter* to call on her magic, but today, the words that tripped of her tongue were new.

"*Aredoma flaria.*"

Her palms tingled and began to glow with a golden aura. Her blood burned in her veins as her magic intensified, sending electric jolts through her, until a powerful bolt of blue light shot out. Brighter and more dazzling than any witchfire she had used before, it encircled the egg, which began to vibrate and bounce around.

After a few moments, a tiny crack appeared.

"It's working!" Hugo cried

Abigail kept it up, unleashing every ounce of magic she had until exhaustion crept into her bones. Gritting her teeth, she pushed herself on until, with a loud crack, the eggshell snapped in half.

Abigail dropped her hands, chest heaving from the effort.

In the center of the shell sat a small Omera. Its ebony hide glistened with sticky goo. It stretched one delicate wing out and then another. It opened its mouth and let out a pitiful cry.

Big Mama leaped to its side, giving it a warm bath with her tongue.

The baby opened its eyes and looked straight at Abigail.

She caught her breath. The Omera's eyes were like twin stars, golden and shimmering.

Fetch approached the baby, ignoring the mother's warning growl. He petted it once on the head and then nodded, as if it was exactly as he expected.

"Odin will be pleased," he said cryptically.

The daddy Omera lifted a groggy head and then screeched at them. Big Mama snapped back, and he settled down but continued to make a rumbling noise in his chest.

"Time to go, kids," Jasper said.

"How? We can't hike down that cliff," Abigail said.

"Yeah, and I'm not wading through that swamp again," Hugo added. "Even if I did trap the viken in quicksand, there are still sneevils and things that crawl in the night."

Abigail looked at Hugo, eyebrows raised. "I can't wait to hear that story. But I think I can get us a ride." She turned to Big Mama.

The Omera snapped her head toward Abigail.

"It's the least you can do," Abigail said, stepping forward to run her hand over the baby. "His daddy can watch over him until you return."

The Omera growled, then turned his head away, as if he couldn't be bothered to argue.

Big Mama gave the baby one last lick, then lifted it gently and put it back in the nest with the other two. She lowered herself, dropping one wing, and Abigail climbed onto her back.

"What are you waiting for?" she asked, grinning at her companions.

Hugo was next to climb on. "Are you sure about this?" he asked, nervously wrapping his arms around her waist.

"Sure, I'm sure."

But Jasper shook his head. "Fetch and I can take the long way around. Don't worry about us. You just get home safely."

"I won't have a home much longer," Abigail said, remembering the contest. "I failed to find and tame a pet creature. Now Endera's going to win."

The Omera launched herself into the air. Abigail thrilled as they dropped down the sheer cliff face. She wrapped her arms around Big Mama's neck as Hugo clung to her waist.

And then Big Mama soared up. They flew over the swamps, brushing the tops of the trees. Hugo filled her in on his adventures until they were outside the Tarkana Fortress. The sun was just beginning to set as the Omera coasted down to land.

"Thanks for the ride," Abigail said, rubbing the creature's scaly nose.

Big Mama chuffed at her and then head-butted her.

"You're welcome," she said with a giggle. "I'm glad I could help."

The Omera gathered her thick legs underneath her and launched up into the golden sky.

"Well, that was an adventure," Hugo said. "Here, I found your sea emerald." He put the necklace around her neck.

"It won't be mine for much longer," Abigail sighed. "Once I fail my ABCs, it will belong to Endera."

# Chapter 23

A gaggle of witchlings waited outside the dormitory, excitedly chattering about the creatures they had captured. In the center of them, Abigail saw Endera looking around, probably trying to find Abigail and see what she had. Keeping to the deepening twilight shadows, Abigail snuck around to the rear of the building and scrambled up the ivy. She crawled in through her window, dropping onto the bed in an exhausted heap.

She was neatly tucked under the covers when Madame Vex opened the door and did a bed check. The woman went to the open window and leaned out. Abigail lay still, feigning sleep.

Mumbling something under her breath, Madame Vex closed the window firmly and left.

Abigail slept soundly the rest of the night, dreaming of starshine.

The next morning, she grimly joined the other girls out in the gardens. They each had their pet with them. Tears stung the backs of her eyes. Even with everything that had happened this year, she didn't want to leave.

Endera stood next to a giant Shun Kara wolf with shaggy black hair. Its long snout jutted from a square head capped by sharp ears standing at attention. With a twitch of its lips, it revealed glistening fangs.

The witchling looked Abigail up and down, searching for her creature. When she saw Abigail was empty handed, she began to gloat.

"Unless you have a worm in your pocket, you're going to be expelled," she said, a smile lighting up her face. "I hope you like taking care of nurslings."

Madame Barbosa clapped her hands.

"Inspection time, girls. Madame Vex and I will observe you with your pet. Our decision will be binding."

They went down the line. *What's the point of waiting?* Abigail thought glumly. She should just pack her bags and leave now.

She must have shifted her feet, because the next second, Endera's voice was in her ear.

"Don't you move," Endera hissed. "You're going to watch me win, and then you're going to hand over that sea emerald."

Abigail just sighed.

Watching over the nurslings would be okay.

She kept repeating that to herself as, one by one, Madame Barbosa oohed and aahed over the creatures. Madame Vex kept her nose in the air, giving a brief nod of her head at each one. Most of the girls had managed to charm shreeks that carried their bookbags. Portia had a pair of shreeks that flew around her head, quickly braiding her hair. Minxie had enchanted a rathos that ate pickled cheese from her hand. Nelly had wrangled a young sneevil that stood up on its back paws. Her hands were bandaged from the pokes of its tiny tusks, but even Madame Vex was impressed.

Next up was a quiet girl named Lucilla. She stood with her head down, hands empty. She sniffled loudly as Madame Vex pointed at the gates.

"Pack your things and go."

The poor witchling dragged herself off.

Abigail sighed. She wouldn't be far behind.

They moved on to Glorian, who had an old shreek with wrinkled graying skin. It snored loudly in its cage, refusing to wake up. Madame Vex just sniffed. "Hardly worth the effort," she said.

Madame Barbosa patted the girl on the shoulder. "A passing grade, dear, but next time, do try harder."

Endera was next.

The witchling stood by her Shun Kara, chest puffed out, looking as proud as the beast. She snapped her fingers, and it growled, baring white fangs that gleamed with hunger.

"My, my," Madame Barbosa purred, reaching out one hand to scratch the beast's ears. "This is a fine specimen. Can you make it do something?"

Endera took a bone from her pocket and threw it in a high arc.

The animal lunged forward and raced in a blur across the clearing, snatching the bone from the air before it hit the ground. It skidded to a stop, tearing a hole in the grass, and then trotted proudly back to Endera's side and dropped it at her feet.

Endera folded her arms and glowed, as if she were already Head Witchling.

Abigail sighed to herself. It wasn't fair. It really wasn't. But still, saving the baby Omera had made her feel . . . good.

She put on a smile as the pair of teachers stopped in front of her.

"Well, Abigail, what have you to show us?" Madame

Barbosa asked, looking over Abigail's shoulder to see if she was hiding a creature.

Abigail opened her mouth to admit she had failed when an ominous shadow flashed across the sky. The sound of rushing wind and beating wings sent a ripple of excitement fluttering through her. It couldn't be. It just couldn't.

But it was.

With a loud thump, Big Mama landed on the grass and shrieked horribly, sending the witchlings screaming for cover.

Madame Barbosa and Madame Vex drew their hands up, ready to send a blast of deadly witchfire, but Abigail threw herself in front of the creature.

"No, don't. She's . . . she's with me," she said. "Surprise!" Abigail scratched Big Mama's scaly black head, and the Omera huffed in pleasure.

"You tamed an . . . an . . . uh . . ." Madame Barbosa was rendered speechless.

Madame Vex's face was ashen. "Send it away, you fool. A wild Omera could kill any of us with an accidental jab of its spiked tail."

Abigail turned and put her arms around Big Mama's neck. "Thank you," she whispered. "You can go home now."

It was probably her imagination, but it looked as if the Omera winked at her. Then it sprang into the sky and winged away.

Abigail turned back to face the staring crowd of girls. "Well, did I win?"

"No, no, no!" Endera shrieked, stomping her foot. "It's not fair. I got a Shun Kara wolf!" The animal howled in support.

"Now, Endera," Madame Barbosa said. "Be a good

sport. I think it's clear who the winner is. Abigail, please come forward and claim your Head Witchling pin."

Abigail stepped up, and Madame Barbosa pinned the prized gold pin, a letter *T* for the Tarkana Academy, to her dress. As the two older witches walked away, still muttering over Abigail's feat, Abigail turned to Endera. The girl had furious tears running down her cheeks.

"I believe you owe me one spellbook," Abigail said, triumphantly holding out her hand.

Endera's lips trembled. The girl reached down into her school bag and pulled out a thin book. It was made of scarred black leather and the pages were yellowed.

Endera held on to it tightly. Her eyes were like daggers as she glared at Abigail. "I swear, Abigail Tarkana, you will regret this." Then she shoved the book into Abigail's hands and stomped off. Her Shun Kara loped after her, followed by Glorian and Nelly.

The rest of the witchlings crowded around Abigail, patting her on the back and cheering her.

Abigail was enjoying every bit of the attention until a prickly feeling ran up her spine.

She turned, searching for the source of her unease. There. Up in the tower. A woman stood in the window, watching her.

Melistra.

Abigail shivered as the powerful witch stared at her.

Suddenly, she wished she had asked for anything but Endera's spellbook.

# Chapter 24

*I must be dreaming*, Abigail decided. Here she was sitting at Yule Day's Eve lunch with all the popular girls, and everyone was hanging on her every word.

The Dining Hall had been decorated with fir tree trimmings and scented pinecones. Candles glittered on every table, adding a festive quality to the room. A fire burned in the hearth, and some of the girls were cooking popcorn.

Ever since she had won the Head Witchling competition, Abigail had been the center of attention. No more eating alone in the corner. No more waiting to be picked for partner in Positively Potent Potions.

No. As Head Witchling of the firstling's class, Abigail was suddenly the queen bee. The belle of the ball. The *it* girl.

"Tell us again, Abby dear, what happened when you met the Omera," Portia asked. The school's most beautiful firstling looked at Abigail with her large teal green eyes, hands clasped in her lap as she waited for Abigail's answer.

"Well, it happened like this . . ."

Abigail launched once more into the tale of how she had come across the black-winged Omera in the swamps and cast her charm spell over it.

Of course, she left out the part where it had kidnapped her and taken her to its nest to help hatch its youngling. She especially left out the part where she had met her father and been filled with starshine.

Because that was hard to explain.

"I know you cheated," a voice snarled.

Abigail didn't have to turn around to know that sour voice had come from Endera.

She let out a dramatic sigh. "Oh, Endera, are you still jealous because I won and took your precious spell-book?" Abigail ran a hand over the thin tome that rested on the table. A shiver ran up her spine.

Truth be told, Abigail hadn't even opened it. The leathery skin quivered under her touch, as if it were alive. She wanted nothing more than to shove the ugly thing deep down in her bookbag, but she wouldn't back down to Endera.

Twin spots of red marked Endera's cheeks as she faced off against Abigail. "Wild Omeras are impossible to charm. So that means you cheated. That book is mine, and I will get it back."

Next to her, Nelly smirked, "I bet she doesn't even know how to *uuuuse* it."

On the other side of Endera, Glorian nodded vigorously. "That's right. She's probably too scared to even open it."

An oily whisper tickled Abigail's ears.

*Do it. Show her. Show them all what you can do, dark witch.*

Abigail's spine tightened, and she found her voice. "Is that so?" she said sweetly. It was time to shut Endera and her pals up for good. "Let's see, shall we?" She opened the book to a random page.

The letters were a blur, but they swam into focus as she pressed her finger down on the parchment and recited the hand-inked words.

"*Gally mordana, gilly pormona, gelly venoma.*"

Her words rang out as a hush fell over the room. Even the upper-level girls sensed a change in the atmosphere. A hundred pairs of eyes turned on Abigail. Dread rushed through her veins.

*What have I done?*

The three witchlings backed away, looking frightened, but before they'd taken two steps, they began to shimmer. Glorian's whole body shook. Nelly's eyes grew wide.

Endera shouted, "No! Take it back!"

But she was too late. With a sucking *gloop*, all three girls disappeared.

There was a moment of shocked silence. And then the Dining Hall erupted into applause.

"Great trick, Abigail," Portia said, clapping her hands in delight.

The applause faded away as she and the other witchlings waited for Abigail to make the girls reappear.

"Go ahead," Portia prompted. "Bring them back now."

Abigail stood frozen in place. The spellbook dangled numbly from her fingers. Her brain couldn't take in what she had just done. That kind of magic was . . . *intoxicating.* Her blood soared, but at the same time she felt nauseous. Sick.

Because not only were Endera and her friends gone, but Abigail had no idea where they were or, more importantly, how to get them back.

The door to the Dining Hall banged open, and Madame Vex swept in, pausing in the entrance. "What is going on?"

She wrinkled her nose, sniffing the air, as if she could smell the traces of the spell Abigail had cast.

The crowd of witchlings around Abigail parted and stepped back.

Swooping down on Abigail, her eyes flared at the sight of the spellbook in her hands.

"Abigail Tarkana, what have you done?"

# Chapter 25

Hugo sat in the jookberry tree, swinging his legs, and checked the time on his pocket watch. Abigail should have been here an hour ago. She had promised she would come, double crossed her heart.

*Who am I kidding?* he thought with a sigh. Abigail had bigger fish to fry now that she was so popular.

In fact, ever since she had won the Head Witchling competition, Abigail had been too busy to spend time with Hugo.

"Sorry, Hugo, but Minxie and the girls want me to show them how I braid my hair," she had said the first day. "Maybe we can hang out tomorrow."

The second day it had been, "Dear Hugo, the most popular girl in school, Portia Tarkana, well, she wants me to teach her how I get this glow to my skin. I promise tomorrow—super swear—I will be there."

Then she'd raced off to join the flock of fawning girls that seemed to follow her everywhere.

Abigail was getting such a big head, it was a miracle she could fit into her uniform.

He should just go home. His mother would be fixing her annual Yule Day fig pudding, and later they would each open a small gift around the fire. That's what he should do. But he and Abigail hadn't learned anything new in ages, and he wanted answers, at the very least to show Abigail he was still useful to have around. He pulled out his notebook, studying the pages of notes.

They now knew Abigail's blue witchfire came from her father. But they still didn't know why Lissandra had been running away and how she had died. Abigail could still be in danger. If he was going to get to the bottom of it, he needed to find out more about Lissandra.

And Hugo had an idea who he could ask.

There was an old witch, an outcast who didn't live behind the walls of the Tarkana Fortress. His brother, Emenor, had warned Hugo about her.

Emenor claimed the witch had put a swine curse on his friend Milton for teasing her. Emenor might not always like Hugo, but he didn't want his only brother to walk around with a pig's tail. It would embarrass him. Poor Milton had never shown his face in school again without hearing oinking squeals behind his back.

Leaving the Tarkana Fortress, Hugo made his way into the lower part of town, away from the nice shops. He was looking for a misshapen lump of rags. That's how Emenor had described the old witch.

*There.*

On the corner across from the stables, an old woman squatted on the ground, a begging bowl in front of her. A long cloak made of old rags hung over her shoulders. She was drawing a circle in the dirt with a sharp stick.

Hugo drew in a breath, clenched his hands into fists for courage, and then walked over to her. He squatted down until he was eye level. There was a single copper in her bowl, a half penny. The witch kept drawing, but her shoulders stiffened as she waited for him to speak.

He reached into his pocket and pulled out the silver coin he'd taken from his Yule stocking that morning, tossing it into the bowl. It clanked loudly. Gnarled fingers flashed out and snatched it up, making it disappear into the bodice of her gown. Only then did she lift her eyes to his.

They were an emerald green so piercing Hugo almost fell backward.

"What do you want?" she snarled.

"I . . . that is, I have a question."

"You seek knowledge from me?" A harsh wheezing sound that might have been laughter shook her body. "I'm naught but a pile of rags. What could I possibly tell you?"

"I want to know what happened to Lissandra," he said.

At the mention of Abigail's mother, the old witch drew back.

"How dare you. Who are you? Who sent you?" Flashing eyes searched the square.

Hugo tried to rise. "I didn't mean . . ."

But before he could explain, she held up her palm and blew a handful of black powder in his face.

The world went blank.

# Chapter 26

Abigail sat on a wooden bench outside Madame Hestera's chambers trembling from head to toe. She was cold. So cold. Ever since she had used that spellbook, it felt as though a sliver of ice had embedded in her heart, sending slush through her veins.

The coven leader held court in a room at the top of the fortress towers. The corridor was lined with portraits of their ancestors. Abigail looked up into the eyes of an ancient witch named Nestra. Her haughty gaze looked down at Abigail as if she knew exactly what the firstling had done.

Abigail wanted to stick her tongue out at the old witch. What did she care if Endera was gone? Served the girl right. She was terrible in every way. And her friends were no better.

*Yes, dark witch, they deserved it.*

She covered her ears, trying to block out that oily voice. It was the spellbook. She could feel it rattling around in her bookbag. Calling out to her, hoping to get her to open it again.

She inched away from it. It was a hateful thing. She wished she could burn it, but then was horrified by the thought.

Vor's words came back to her.

*Don't let the darkness win.*

Bile rose up in Abigail, choking her with guilt.

"What have I done?" she whispered.

"Are you all right?"

Abigail jumped, startled by the interruption, then was relieved to see a familiar face. "Calla! What are you doing here?"

"I heard you were in trouble. Sorry I was so mean."

"That's okay. I'm sorry, too. Friends?" Abigail stuck her hand out.

Calla nodded, shaking it firmly.

"Did you really use the spellbook on Endera?"

Before Abigail could answer, the door to Madame Hestera's chambers opened.

Madame Vex stood in the doorway, looking down her thin nose, and crooked a finger at Abigail.

Abigail rose, wishing she could make herself disappear.

"It'll be okay." Calla smiled encouragingly. She picked up Abigail's book bag and held it out.

"You think so?" Abigail reached for it, but Calla held on and leaned in to whisper in her ear. "My great-aunt's not as mean as she looks. If she were, I wouldn't be here."

She gave Abigail a wink, pushing the bag into her hands, and then Madame Vex dragged Abigail inside the room and slammed the door shut.

Madame Hestera was seated on a high-backed chair in front of a fireplace. One hand rested on her emerald-tipped cane. A woman stood staring out the window, her back to Abigail.

Melistra.

Abigail's heart began to drum so loud it was a wonder the chandelier didn't shake.

Madame Vex cleared her throat. "Abigail, explain to Madame Hestera what kind of spell you used on those witchlings."

Before Abigail could open her mouth, Madame Hestera leaned forward, rapping her cane on the stone floor. "You realize, child, causing harm to a fellow witch is an offense punishable by exile."

Abigail's knees went weak and she swayed. Exile? That meant being kicked out of the coven, stripped of your magic, and sent away. Better off being a glitch-witch than an exile. She couldn't bear it.

"I'm sorry," she blurted out. "I didn't mean it. Endera was teasing me, and I . . . I just read off the first spell I saw."

Endera's mother turned slowly to face her. Her eyes were blazing coals of emerald fire. "You had no right to use my spellbook," she hissed. She raised her hand clenching her fingers in the empty air.

Abigail froze as all breath left her body.

"I'm—suh—suh—" she gasped, trying to find air as invisible fingers of power gripped her throat, cutting off her supply of oxygen.

"Tell me what spell you used," she commanded. "Speak!"

Abigail's throat loosened enough for her to form words. "It started with *gally mordana*."

Melistra paled. "You sent my daughter to the netherworld. You should die in flames this instant. You should be turned into a pile of cinders and ash." She raised her hand again, as if to deliver the fatal strike. Abigail had no strength to even move.

"Stop!" Madame Vex said, stepping forward to shield Abigail. "The girl meant no harm. You heard her. She didn't know what she was doing. How is it your spellbook came into her hands, Melistra?"

Melistra looked angry enough to explode. Before she could utter a word, Hestera drove her cane into the ground.

"Enough squabbling. You are both right. Melistra, your spellbook is too powerful to be in the hands of a firstling. Madame Vex, mind your words. Melistra is a High Witch. She will have your respect."

Madame Vex was the first to give in, tilting her chin at Melistra and taking a step away from Abigail. It took another agonizing moment, and then Melistra released Abigail from the choking spell.

"Give me the spellbook so I can find the return spell and bring my daughter and those half-wits back," she snapped, holding out her hand.

Relief shot through Abigail. A solution! Melistra would find the right spell and bring them back. Abigail was so excited, she nearly dropped her bag searching for the spellbook.

*Where is it?*

She pushed aside her Magical Maths book and her Potions journal. It had to be here. She hadn't taken it out. All eyes were on her as Abigail searched harder.

No one had touched her book bag except for her.

She blinked. That wasn't true. Calla had touched it. The cunning glitch-witch had picked up her bag, leaned in close, and whispered in her ear. She must have taken it. But why?

"Um, I don't have it," Abigail said.

Melistra's eyes flashed fire as she raised a threatening hand. Madame Vex moved in front of Abigail once again.

"The girl will be locked in her room until she produces the book," she said.

There was a tense silence.

Madame Hestera finally nodded. "If the book is not returned by the end of day tomorrow, she will be brought in front of the High Witch Council and charged with crimes against another witchling. Endera and the other two won't survive long in the netherworld."

"Not against that horrid eight-legged monster," Melistra agreed, spearing Abigail with the hatred that blazed from her eyes.

# Chapter 27

Hugo swam back to consciousness to find the world a blurry kaleidoscope. He removed his glasses, wiping off smudges of black powder, then put them back on.

Better.

He sat up. He was in a shack of some kind. Sunlight poked through holes in the roof and a rickety door hung half-off its latch.

"Hello?" he croaked. His mouth was dry, as if he had swallowed a ball of cotton.

Smoke rose from a small fireplace, where a cauldron rested over the coals. Dried herbs hung from the ceiling. A table held jars of what looked like various sizes of pickled eyeballs.

*Gross.*

He tried to get up, then realized his feet were bound with rope. He bent to untie them, but when he touched the twine, a spark jumped out and shocked him.

They were enchanted. That witch had done this to him, taken him prisoner and spirited him back to her lair.

But why?

Hugo had heard stories of what witches did to stray kids that wandered into their traps. Turned them into creatures. Trained them as their pets.

He wasn't about to let that happen. Getting to his feet, he began hopping to the door. He had only made it three hops when the door was flung open, and a young girl stood framed in the doorway.

Her hair was lighter than Abigail's raven locks, almost brunette. Her large eyes sparkled with excitement. She was carrying a school bag over her shoulder. Her mouth dropped open in surprise as Hugo hopped toward her.

"Who are you?" she asked.

"I'm Hugo. Who are you?"

"Oh, you're Abigail's Balfin friend. Nice to meet you. I'm Calla. But why are you hopping?"

Hugo looked pointedly down at his feet, and she groaned.

"Baba Nana, untie this boy immediately."

Baba Nana? Did this girl know the horrid witch who'd kidnapped him and tied him up like a hog?

A wheezy laugh came from behind a ragged curtain. The curtain was thrust aside, and Baba Nana waddled out.

"Now, child, calm yourself. Baba Nana was only having a bit of fun."

There was a loud crackle, and the ropes around Hugo's feet disappeared.

"You know this witch?" he said, still outraged over his treatment.

Calla smiled. "Of course. She's my godmother. She's taken care of me forever." The girl moved over to a small stove and put a kettle on. "Would you care for some tea?" she asked, as if it were perfectly natural for Hugo to be in this hovel.

"No, I'd like to go home," he said, edging toward the door. But a zing of witchfire made him jump back.

"You cannot leave until you tell me why you were asking about Lissandra," the old witch snarled.

"Now, Baba Nana, be nice. I have good news," Calla said. "I've got it!"

"Got what, child?"

"Melistra's book of spells." She pulled a leather-bound book out of her bag and held it up.

Baba Nana crowed with delight. "Wonderful. But how ever did you get your hands on that?"

"Wait a minute." Hugo recognized that book. "You took Abigail's spellbook."

She clutched the book to her chest. "Well, it's a good thing I did. She's in a heap of trouble."

"What do you mean?" Hugo's heart lurched. If Abigail was in trouble, she would need his help.

"Abigail used the book to send Endera and two other witchlings to the netherworld. She was called up to Madame Hestera's chambers to face the consequences. I took it from her before she went in."

"Calla, you shouldn't have interfered," Baba Nana scolded. "That spellbook belongs to Melistra. She could have used it to bring those witchlings back."

Calla blinked rapidly, her eyes shiny with tears. "But I had to. This book is going to help me get my magic."

"*Might* help you, child," Baba Nana said, sounding kinder than Hugo would have guessed possible. "Baba Nana doesn't know if she can find the right spell in there. It may be no magic can undo the curse you've got."

"Curse?" Now Hugo was interested. He pulled out his notebook. "What curse?"

"The glitch-witch curse," Calla said. "It stops me from getting my powers. I know I have magic. I can feel it at times. But something is blocking it."

"No time for that now," Baba Nana said. "Every second we delay, those three witchlings are closer to death. We must bring them back before something terrible happens, or your friend will pay the price with exile."

"We'll need Abigail's help," Hugo said.

Calla shook her head. "She's been locked inside her room. The door will be guarded. There's no way we can sneak past them."

"Then we'll have to find another way." Hugo chewed on his pencil, looking over his notes, and then paused. It was a crazy idea, but maybe . . . just maybe, it would work.

"We'll need an Omera," he announced.

Baba Nana's eyes widened. "Have you lost your mind, child? An Omera will tear your head off."

Hugo grinned. "Not if you call the right one."

# Chapter 28

endera shivered. Something heavy lay across her stomach. She poked at it and received a groan in response.

"Where are we?" Nelly asked groggily.

"I don't know," Endera said, giving the girl a push. All she remembered was spinning blackness and splintered ice that filled her bones, then this place. She sat up. Glorian lay sprawled out next to her. She gave the witchling a nudge. "Wake up, Glorian."

"What's happened?" Glorian asked, holding one hand to her head.

"That stupid Abigail used magic on us." Endera practically spat out the words.

Powerful magic.

"So where did we go?" Nelly asked again.

Endera wished she had an answer—something simple like "Rotten Abigail sent us down into the dungeons." Easy enough. Or "The dirty fink transported us into the swamps." They could walk home. But this place . . . this place felt different. Otherworldly.

Endera took a good look around.

Wisps of fog made it hard to see things clearly in the murky light. She could just make out solid rock walls surrounding them.

"Hello?"

Her voice echoed in the chamber.

"Is anyone there?" Glorian added.

A scraping noise made them go still. It was as if someone, or something, had run a long nail across a stone.

"I've got magic, and I'm not afraid to use it," Endera called out, though her voice cracked a little.

"Yeah, we've got *maaaagic*," Nelly called out in her nastiest voice. "Witch magic."

The grating noise came again, as if something was dragging itself out of a corner.

"Deliccciousss," a voice whispered.

Murmured echoes of the word surrounded them, as if a crowd had gathered.

"We're not delicious," Endera shouted. "I'm sour, and Nelly's tough as Gomaran steel."

Where were the voices coming from? They seemed to echo from every corner of the chamber.

"Mmmm, methinks so."

The whisper drifted through the mist, followed by the sound of clawing nails as the unseen beast dragged itself closer to Endera. She could almost feel its hot breath on her neck.

"W-we th-th-thinks not," Endera stuttered as fear wrapped her throat in a tight grip. She thrust her palm toward the noise, sending a burst of witchfire.

It sputtered harmlessly against stone.

The three girls inched closer together until they stood with their backs to each other.

"Show yourself. Don't be a coward," Endera snapped.

"Ssssooo hungry," the voice rasped from behind her.

Endera whirled around, sending a wild spurt of witch-fire over Nelly's shoulder.

"Where is it?" she asked.

"It was there, I swear," Nelly said. "I heard it."

Endera waved one hand, trying to wipe away the mist that fogged her vision. All she could make out were craggy stone walls on all sides.

Unless . . . she tilted her head back and looked up, shrieking.

Directly over their heads were dozens of fat spiders hanging on glimmering threads, spinning lazily in the dim light. Their purplish-black bodies were the size of large pumpkins. Their multiple sets of eyes glittered with hunger as they eyed the three witchlings.

Nelly and Glorian followed her gaze, screaming in unison.

"Endera, what do we do?" Nelly asked once she'd stopped her screaming.

Endera's mind raced. "My mother will come get us. I know she will. We just have to wait for her to get here."

Webbing crisscrossed the chamber overhead. It went up several stories.

"Leave us alone," Endera shouted. "We are Tarkana witches. The Great Mother spider is our guardian. You may not harm us."

"*Harrrrm* you?"

One of the spiders lowered itself down on a thin strand of web until it was eye level with her. It had a large set of eyes in the center of its head, then three smaller pairs around it, all looking at her. "Did we say *harrrrm* you?"

Two more spiders lowered themselves in front of Glorian and Nelly.

Endera blinked, seeing herself in its many eyes. Dizziness swamped her. Nelly and Glorian swayed next to her. "You . . . you said you were hungry. That we were delicious."

The spider held her gaze. "And so you *arrrre*." And then it tilted its body, and a spray of silk strands surrounded Endera.

The other two spiders did the same to Glorian and Nelly.

Endera screamed once, and then silken webbing silenced her.

# Chapter 29

Abigail paced inside her room, guilt lancing her every step. She hadn't just sent those witchlings away; she had condemned them to certain death at the hands of some monster with eight legs. And now Calla had the spellbook and Abigail had no idea where to find her. If only she had kept her big mouth shut, she wouldn't be in this mess.

She stopped pacing. It was no good beating herself up. She had to fix this, and to do that, she had to get out of this room, find Calla, and get that spellbook back.

Throwing a cloak on, she flung open the window, ready to climb down the ivy, and gasped.

Someone had cut the vines away from her sill.

*Madame Vex.*

She must have guessed Abigail had snuck in that way. Closing the window, Abigail sank to the ground, wrapping her arms around her knees. She would never get out of her room now. Those girls were as good as dead, and she would be exiled from the coven forever. The thought brought tears to her eyes.

Something pinged against her window. A surge of hope shot through her.

She leaped to her feet and flung open the window. "Hugo!"

Hugo sat on the back of Big Mama, who hovered silently. Calla clung to his waist, looking terrified.

"Care for a lift?" Hugo asked calmly, as if riding on the back of an Omera were an everyday occurrence.

"I would," she said. She climbed onto the ledge and took his hand. He pulled her on in front of him. She had barely settled when Big Mama flapped her wings and soared away.

Abigail wanted to whoop with joy at the feeling of flying over the rooftops of the Tarkana Fortress.

Hugo guided the Omera to a clearing on the edge of the swamps near the far end of Jadewick.

She glimpsed a small shack in the thick swamp before Big Mama swooped down and landed. She slid off the Omera's back, rushing forward to give the creature's nose a rub. "How are your babies?" she asked, as the other two jumped down.

Big Mama nudged her and gave an eye roll.

Abigail laughed. "A handful, I'm sure. Tell Waxer I said hello, and tell Vexer to stay out of trouble. Give Starfire a kiss for me."

The Omera snorted, then launched herself into the air and took flight.

Abigail turned and gave Hugo a firm hug. "How on earth did you get Big Mama to help you?"

"I whistled like this," Hugo put two fingers between his teeth and trilled off key, then grinned ruefully. "But nothing happened. Baba Nana used a spell to call her. Big Mama almost ate us when she landed, but then I told her you needed help. It's strange how she understands things."

Abigail turned to Calla. "You took Melistra's spellbook. Do you know how much trouble I'm in because of you? If I don't get that spellbook back by the end of the day, I'm going to be exiled from the coven."

Calla paled. "I'm sorry, Abigail. It was selfish of me. But don't worry, Baba Nana will help us fix it."

"Who's Baba Nana?" Abigail asked, but Calla was already hurrying toward the rundown shack.

"It's her godmother," Hugo said. "She's going to use the spellbook to help Calla break the curse on her."

Abigail frowned. "What curse?"

"The glitch-witch curse. Hurry! We don't have much time."

Inside the shack, Abigail blinked, her eyes adjusting to the dim interior. The place was a mess. Dishes were stacked up in the sink. Dust clung to every surface. A small rathos scurried across the floor, disappearing into a hole in the wall.

An old woman with frizzy gray hair was huddled over a table. Her face was as wrinkled and dry as a prune. Her clothes were nothing more than a heap of rags.

Melistra's spellbook was open before her. She was muttering to herself, running her finger down a page.

*Hellooo, dark witch.*

Abigail started at the whispered greeting. She glanced around, but no one else had heard it. The spellbook seemed to call out only to her. Her fingers itched to hold it.

*Yes, come closer. Such power in you.*

The old woman slammed the book shut, raising her eyes to zero in on Abigail. "You're the witchling that used the spellbook. Don't you know how dangerous it is?"

"I didn't think. I just . . . Glorian said I couldn't use it and . . ."

Baba Nana snorted. "So you had to prove her wrong. Just like your mother. Lissandra was always so stubborn."

"Sorry, Abigail," Hugo said. "I had to tell her the truth to get her to help us."

"You knew my mother?" Abigail asked.

Baba Nana waved her hand. "Not now, child. We need to bring those witchlings back."

"Then give me the spellbook," Abigail said. "I'll take it to Melistra and she'll fix this."

Baba Nana shook her head. "There's no time, child. Every minute we delay, your friends are closer to death. And if they die, you will be like me. Banished forever."

Abigail drew closer. "So how do we reverse the spell?"

"It won't be easy. You sent those witchlings to the netherworld."

"The netherworld?" Hugo asked. "Where is that?"

"It's where banished creatures are sent by the gods," Baba Nana explained. "It's ruled over by the Arachnia, a race of nasty ravenous spiders. Their queen is Octonia, an eight-legged beast who can suck your insides dry. They will most likely have captured the witchlings by now. You'll have to go there, find them, and convince Octonia to release them."

"How can we do that?" Abigail asked, thinking it sounded hopeless.

Baba Nana paced. "Your only hope is to outwit Octonia. Trade her something she wants more than your little friends."

"Like what?" Hugo asked.

"We'll have to think of something more tempting than

three young witchlings," Baba Nana mused. "The Arachnia are ravenous things but not very smart. As I recall, Queen Octonia is very full of herself." The old witch rummaged around her counter, knocking over jars, and then lifted a handheld mirror. She spat on it and polished the glass. "She's just vain enough that this might work," she muttered.

"A mirror?" Abigail asked doubtfully.

Baba Nana shoved it in her hands. "It's up to you to convince her it's a worthwhile trade. When you have your friends, don't hesitate. You must recite the return spell, *dominus delirias daloros*, three times."

Abigail tucked the mirror into the pocket of her cloak, reciting the words to herself.

"I'm coming with you," Hugo said.

"And me," Calla added. "This is partly my fault. I want to help."

As much as she wanted the company, Abigail couldn't risk her friend's lives. "No, it's too dangerous, Hugo. You don't have any magic. And sorry, Calla, neither do you."

"Doesn't matter. I'm coming," Hugo said. "You'll need help."

"And I am too, so it's settled." Calla was pale but firm. She took Hugo's hand in hers and held her other hand out to Abigail.

Abigail hesitated. "Are you sure?"

Calla clasped her hand, squeezing it tightly. "It will be my first adventure. Come on, Baba Nana, cast the spell and we'll be off."

"Be careful, child." The old woman stepped closer and put one gnarled hand on Calla's cheek. "You're all this old witch has to care about in the world."

"I will. Just, please, while we're gone, try to find something in that book that can help break the glitch-witch curse," Calla said.

Baba Nana gave a nod and then licked her lips, looking at Abigail.

"Are you ready?"

Abigail nodded.

Baba Nana lifted the spellbook and began reciting the words.

"*Gally mordana, gilly pormona, gelly venoma.*"

A tingle ran up Abigail's spine, and then a sharp wind blew in her face. Ice filled the marrow in her bones, and then blackness engulfed her.

# Chapter 30

"Where are we?" Calla asked.

Hugo sat up. Solid rock rose up on every side. A light mist hung in the chilly air. Definitely not Baba Nana's hovel.

"The netherworld, I suppose," he said. "But how do we get out of here?"

"Up there," Abigail said, pointing.

Hugo looked up. A mass of thankfully empty webbing crisscrossed the shaft.

"It looks like we'll be climbing," he said briskly.

"I wish I'd never opened that stupid spellbook," Abigail sighed.

"What's done is done," Hugo said. "Now we have to fix it." He tested the strands. "It's sticky, but I think it will hold us."

Hugo went first. Spider silk clung to his hair and face. He kept brushing it away, but soon his hands were a mess, and his clothes were streaked with webbing.

The two girls followed close behind. No one complained, though their arms ached by the time they finally reached the top and stepped onto a wide ledge. They brushed off the webbing that clung to their hair and clothes and took a look around. A pair of tunnels led in opposite directions.

"Which way?" Calla asked.

They listened, but there was only silence.

Hugo pointed to the right. "I say we take this one and see where it leads. If it's a dead end, we'll come back and try the other one."

"I say we split up," Abigail said. "We'll cover more ground. You and Calla stick together."

Hugo hesitated, but Abigail had already hurried off down the first tunnel.

"Give a whistle if you run into trouble," he called.

Abigail seemed worried. Or guilty. He could understand that, but it wasn't really her fault. It's not like she'd meant to harm those witchlings.

"Come on," he said to Calla.

They began to walk down the other tunnel, carefully picking their way around rocks. The air was cold, but there was just enough light to see. Water dripped from the ceiling, occasionally splatting him with cold drops. Strands of webbing clung to the walls. He kept expecting giant spiders to leap out at them.

They came upon another chamber that went down several stories. This one had spiders actively spinning webs. They tiptoed past and didn't make a sound until they were well away.

"Do you think we'll find them in time?" Calla asked.

"I hope so."

"I should have never taken the spellbook," Calla said, wringing her hands.

The scientist in him couldn't argue with that. "True. Melistra would have brought them home already."

Her face crumpled, and snuffled tears followed.

They walked in silence while Hugo searched for the right thing to say.

"If I had a chance to get magic, I probably would have taken it too."

Calla smiled weakly, swiping her tears away with her sleeve. "Thanks. But it looks like we've wasted our time."

Hugo looked up to see they'd come to a dead end. Tumbled rocks blocked their passage. They would have to turn around and hope Abigail had had better luck.

They turned to go, when a faint breeze tickled Hugo's face. He paused, turning back to study the barrier.

"There might be an opening somewhere," he said. "Help me move some of these rocks."

They strained to shove and lift the stones out of the way. After a few minutes, a small opening appeared.

"Stay back," Hugo warned in a low voice. "There could be an army of spiders waiting." He carefully crawled forward on hands and knees.

"What do you see?" Calla whispered. "Spiders?"

"No. It's . . . They're beautiful!"

Calla squeezed in behind him.

"Oh, my!"

They stood up and gawked.

They were perched on a ledge inside a giant cavern. The ceiling was lit up with crystals that glowed faintly like scattered stars. Below them, a pond was lined with giant ferns. Purple insects zoomed across the water. Their double set of wings fluttered rapidly as they skimmed over the surface. Their bodies were as long as Hugo was tall.

"They're dragonflies!" Calla said. "Really, really big ones."

"What are they doing here?" Hugo asked.

"Maybe we can ask them for help. They might know how to get the witchlings away from the Arachnia."

Before Hugo could stop her, she gave a little shout.

"Hello there! We're friends in need of help."

Instantly all the fluttering halted. A swarm of insects lifted off the ground in unison and began arrowing toward them, buzzing loudly.

Hugo stepped back. "Uh, Calla, I think that was a bad idea."

"Nonsense. They're dragonflies. They won't hurt us."

But no sooner had she spoken than the lead dragonfly opened its jaws, revealing a small set of sharp teeth. It looked as if it was aiming to bite Calla's head off.

Hugo tackled Calla, knocking her to the side.

"Stop!" he shouted. "We're here to defeat Queen Octonia!"

The swarm of dragonflies hesitated, hovering in midair.

The lead dragonfly settled down onto the ledge. Its eyes were large bulbous things that reflected Hugo's image in their metallic depths.

Twin sets of sheer wings fluttered delicately. Its body was purple-green with tinges of blue. A golden crown sprouted from its head, as if it were molded onto the dragonfly's body.

"Who sent you?" His voice was deep, commanding, as if he was used to being obeyed.

"No one. Some witchlings were sent here by accident," Hugo said. "We've come to rescue them from Queen Octonia."

"Impossible!" the regal dragonfly said. "Queen Octonia is invincible. You must go, or we will all die!"

# Chapter 31

Abigail made her way down the tunnel, wrapping her cloak tight around her. The place smelled musty and damp, like rotting bones. She had been walking for what felt like hours, but the tunnel stretched on in an endless line. By now, Queen Octonia had probably devoured the witchlings and was ready for a fresh set to swallow.

*Might as well eat me,* Abigail thought glumly. Anything was better than exile.

With one spell, she had thrown away her future. She would never be a great witch now. She wouldn't be a witch at all.

Abigail halted, gulping back the pain.

They would strip her magic. She looked at her hands, wondering if it would hurt.

But was it any worse than what the witchlings she had sent here had endured?

Tears blurred her eyes as she continued on. She had no business feeling sorry for herself. This was all her fault. The tunnel began to climb upward, and she came to a stone archway carved with a spider over the top.

Queen Octonia's lair.

Abigail carefully peered around the opening.

A giant cavern spread out before her. Shiny black spiders crawled along a web that stretched from side to side. In the middle of the cavern, three large objects hung suspended in webbing, wrapped in white silk, like bundles of cotton.

Abigail looked down. Far below, on the bottom of the cavern, scattered bones made an ominous pattern. A draft blew upward, making the web sway.

Near the top, a monstrously large spider sat on a ledge. It was larger than an Omera and twice as wide.

*That must be Queen Octonia.*

Piles of fuzzy gray balls were heaped up in a squirming pile behind her.

Eggs, Abigail realized with a shudder.

A pair of spiders began rolling one of the still figures across the web over to the queen. The giant spider reached one hairy leg out and pawed the stiff form.

"Mmmm!" The fat spider buried her face in the silky bundle, as if she was inhaling its smell. "Delicious and fresh . . . Your queen is pleased."

The Arachnia queen rolled the girl closer and bared a pair of glistening fangs, ready to bite down on the bundled witchling.

"Not so fast!" Abigail shouted, shooting a blast of witchfire across the chasm. It bounced off the queen's backside and a high-pitched *shriek* echoed off the walls.

"Intruder!" the queen bellowed. "Kill her!"

Immediately, the colony of spiders began skittering nimbly across the web toward Abigail, repeating the queen's words over and over in a loud chorus.

"*Kill her. Kill her.*"

Abigail held a ball of flickering witchfire over her palm. "Come near me and I will incinerate that pile of eggs." She launched the warning blast across the top of the squirming gray balls.

"Stop!" The queen commanded, and the approaching spiders froze. She moved in front of the eggs. "Don't you dare harm my beautiful babies."

Abigail held another ball of witchfire. "Give me my friends back and we'll leave you in peace."

The queen clacked her jaws, waving a leg at the colony of spiders. "Why would I give them back when I have so many mouths to feed?"

"Because I have something to trade, a special gift for you much better than some scrawny witchlings."

The queen was silent. Abigail held her breath, waiting to see if she would take the bait.

"A gift you say?" Her mandibles clicked with excitement. "I do love surprises. Come closer so I might see this gift."

The Arachnia promptly spread out, forming a bobbing line that led from the opening where Abigail stood to the giant spider's perch. She let the witchfire go out and took a wobbling step onto the back of the first Arachnia. She stepped from spider to spider, using their hard torsos as stepping stones.

Too soon, she reached the ledge where the queen sat. Octonia had six pairs of eyes, every one of them studying Abigail. Tiny newborn spiders crawled all over the giant Arachnia's body. Queen Octonia affectionately moved the hatchlings about.

"How delicious of you to enter my realm." She leaned in closer. "Such a fresh young thing. My hatchlings will enjoy feasting on you."

"I demand that you release my friends," Abigail said boldly. "The Tarkana witches have the Great Mother spider as their totem."

The spider waved one hairy leg at her. "The Great Mother has forgotten us. We live here in the nothingness, neither here nor there. Why would we care what she thinks?"

Abigail gave a little shrug. "Then I suppose you don't want to hear about how much she misses you and wishes you'd come for a visit. She sent along a very special gift just for you, but if you don't want it, go ahead. Eat me." She closed her eyes and waited.

There was a soft rasp as the queen slid closer. "Show me this gift," she crooned. "It must be valuable for the Great Mother to send you all this way."

Abigail almost smiled. Baba Nana was right. The Arachnia weren't very smart.

She opened her eyes. "Well, the Great Mother said you were the most beautiful spider in all the realms."

"I am?" The queen sounded awed. "I knew it, of course, but to have the Great Mother say it . . ."

"She sent you a gift so you could see for yourself." Abigail began to pull out the mirror, then hesitated. "If I give it to you, you have to promise to let us go home so we can tell her how you liked her gift."

Queen Octonia waved one leg impatiently. "Yes, yes, I give you my word." Her eyes flashed hungrily. "Show me now before I change my mind and devour you."

"First I'm going to free my friends."

Abigail sent witchfire over the cocooned figure at the feet of Octonia, cutting away the thick webbing.

Endera sat up, ripping at the silky wisps and gasping for air as she looked around.

"Mother? Did you come for me?" When she saw Abigail, her face curdled with rage. "You! This is all your fault. I swear, I will get you for this."

"Just play along," Abigail whispered. "You have to trust me. Go free Glorian and Nelly."

Endera peeled off the rest of her cocoon and backed away, stomping angrily across the thick webbing. A few quick blasts of witchfire and the other two witchlings were out of their cocoons.

"Is it lunchtime?" Glorian moaned, wiping away sticky strands.

"I . . . I think we're about to be lunch." Nelly's normally nasty voice quivered with fear.

Abigail turned back to the queen. "And now your majesty, here is the gift sent by the Great Mother." She pulled the mirror out with a flourish.

The spider murmured in delight. "What deliciousness is this?" She reached out a leg and snatched the object, holding it up close and moving it around to all her eyes. "Such beauty! Such perfection!"

"So we can go then," Abigail said. She backed away, stepping across the webbing until she joined the other three witchlings.

"This will never work," Endera spat. "I say we start blasting them."

"No, just keep backing away," Abigail said.

They stepped backward, making their way toward the tunnel entrance.

And then Queen Octonia chuckled. The sound echoed in the giant cavern as she gave a great belly laugh. She tossed the mirror aside and began to crawl across the web toward them. It swayed with her weight.

"You didn't really think I would let you go, did you? Why do you think the Great Mother banished me here in the first place? Because she was jealous of my beauty. So I know she didn't send me that mirror. Which means you're lying."

"I told you it wouldn't work," Endera said, backing away.

The queen crawled closer, her eyes roving over the foursome. "I must say, you're the freshest morsels we've had come along in ages. Better than those sour dragonflies we've been stuck dining on for all these centuries."

# Chapter 32

Hugo and Calla were seated under a giant fern. The dragonflies had carried them down to a mossy clearing. There were several cocoons clinging to the underside of the fronds. Dragonflies perched on every bough, listening in while their leader, King Karran, explained how they had come to be in the netherworld.

"Our colony was sent here eons ago," he began. "We were banished to the netherworld by Odin for biting the neck of his wife Queen Freya. It was a mistake," he explained. "My great-great-grandfather thought Freya was going to kill his mate, but she was just admiring her beauty. Odin exiled our entire colony."

"That sounds terrible," Hugo said, "but we really need your help. We're looking for some witchlings. My friend cast a spell and sent them here. If we don't get them back, she'll be exiled from her coven, just like you were exiled."

"That's not any business of ours. I suggest you leave this place as quickly as possible before the Arachnia find you and you join in their fate."

"But she'll kill them if we don't rescue them," Hugo said.

"You think we don't know that?" King Karran's wings bristled. "We barricade ourselves in here, but those nasty Arachnia burrow in through the walls. They steal our younglings, and we can't stop them."

Calla leaned forward. "Then why not fight back—show them you won't take it anymore?"

The royal dragonfly hung his head. "We tried that many years ago," he said softly. "We mounted an attack. We lost many dragonflies that day. There are too many of them. We have no hope of winning."

"You can't give up," Calla said. "You have to keep trying. Everyone tells me I'm just a glitch-witch with no powers, but I'll never give up trying to get my magic."

"Calla's right," Hugo said. "You must stand up for yourself, or they're going to keep on destroying your colony. Please, help us."

The dragonflies in the ferns began buzzing loudly. Karran nodded his head several times as he listened. Finally, he said, "The colony has spoken. We accept that we cannot defeat the Arachnia."

Hugo sagged. So that was it. They were on their own.

"But we can help you rescue your friends," Karran added. "Then perhaps the gods will see fit to forgive us and release us from this place."

# Chapter 33

Abigail's attempt at rescuing Endera and her side-kicks was not going well. In fact, things had gone from bad to worse.

Queen Octonia loomed over them, snapping her pincers. Poisonous venom dripped from her fangs.

"I should blast you to bits," Endera sniped, glancing angrily at Abigail. "Turn you into a pile of ashes."

"I get it, you're mad," Abigail said. "But right now, we have to focus."

The spiders were drawing closer on every side. The web strained to hold their weight and Queen Octonia's.

Nelly and Glorian spat witchfire, scattering any spider that got too close.

"What's the plan, Endera?" Nelly asked.

"Yeah, you've always got something up your sleeve," Glorian added.

"Just use the spellbook and take us home," Endera snapped at Abigail, sending twin blasts at a hissing spider.

"I don't have it."

"What? Then why are you here?"

"I know the spell to get home," Abigail said. "But we can't leave Hugo and Calla behind."

Endera snorted in disbelief. "Hugo and Calla? You don't mean that smelly Balfin boy that follows you around? What can he do? And Calla is a glitch-witch, what good is she? I say take us home now!"

Nelly and Glorian chimed in their support.

"You know what? I'm starting to think I should have left you wrapped up in that cocoon," Abigail muttered.

"Enough chatter," Queen Octonia purred. "Which one of you would like to be devoured first? Perhaps the plump one." She shot out a blob of webbing at Glorian, but Endera moved fast. She zapped the clump, disintegrating it to ash.

"Say the spell, Abigail, or we're doomed."

Endera was right. Any second, the spiders would overcome them. The web swayed as they were steadily surrounded.

The web. That was it.

"We have to send our witchfire down at the webbing," she said softly.

"What?" Endera looked at Abigail as if she were crazy. "But we'll fall and break our necks."

"You want to stay here and have them suck your bones dry? Go ahead. I say we get rid of Octonia once and for all."

Endera grumbled but didn't object. The four witchlings began blasting the webbing, burning great swaths of it.

Octonia realized the danger too late. She squealed as the web collapsed.

Abigail grabbed onto dangling strands, trying to stop her fall. The webbing slipped from her fingers and the ground came zooming into view. Surely, they were going to smash into a pile of broken bones.

A buzzing sound came from below them, and a swarm of purplish insects appeared from a tunnel. At the front was the largest dragonfly Abigail had ever seen. It wore a golden crown, but the strangest thing by far was the person who rode on its back.

Hugo.

Calla appeared riding on the back of another dragonfly and flew it directly under Abigail.

"I've got you," Calla said, grabbing her. Abigail landed with a thud on its back.

The other three girls each landed on a dragonfly. Glorian sent hers into a nosedive, but it fluttered its wings mightily and evened out.

"Hugo, you rescued us!" Abigail said.

"Calla helped," Hugo said, blushing. "Abigail, meet King Karran."

"No time for chitchat. Let's get out of here," Endera said, turning her dragonfly toward the tunnel.

For once Abigail agreed with her, especially since her plan to destroy Octonia had failed. The spiders had quickly shot out webbing to save their queen, who dangled safely in the web above them.

"After them," Octonia bellowed as the dragonfly squadron headed for the tunnel. The army of spiders dropped like rocks to the floor of the cavern.

Hugo and the girls whizzed down the tunnel on the backs of their dragonflies. Behind them, the skittering, clicking sounds of spiders giving chase bounced off the walls. After some daredevil flying at breakneck speed, they emerged into a large cavern. The dragonflies pulled up, fluttering and trembling with exhaustion as the kids dismounted.

"What now, Hugo?" Abigail said.

"Use your magic to block the tunnel."

Abigail lined up with Endera, Glorian, and Nelly. They began blasting the entrance with bright bursts of witchfire. The clattering sounds of the spiders got closer. Abigail could see their red eyes glowing in the darkness. The tunnel wasn't crumbling.

"Come on, everyone, more!" Abigail cried.

Endera dug her feet in and sent out twin blasts, grunting with effort. Each girl gave it everything she had, but it still wasn't enough. A pair of spiders burst into the cavern.

Hugo and Calla were ready, pelting rocks at the intruders and driving them back into the tunnel. Finally, with a loud crash, boulders tumbled over the entrance, sealing off the horde of Arachnia.

The witchlings dropped their hands, spent.

King Karran landed next to them.

"Thank you," Hugo said. "I will make sure Odin hears of your bravery."

The majestic dragonfly nodded his head gravely, and then he and his subjects lifted as one and flew out of the chamber.

"Let's go home," Calla said.

Abigail began to recite the return spell.

"*Dominus delirias daloros.*"

Cold air swirled around them.

"*Dominus delirias daloros,*" she repeated.

Abigail's skin tingled with electricity.

She opened her mouth to repeat the spell a third time, but before she could get the words out, Queen Octonia burst out of the tunnel, sending rocks flying.

"Going somewhere?" she cried.

Fangs glinting, the giant spider lunged straight for Endera, but the witchling pulled Calla in front of her. Octonia bit down on Calla's arm, quickly backing away and dragging her into the tunnel.

"Calla!" Hugo picked up another rock and heaved it at one of Queen Octonia's eyes. The spider screamed, releasing Calla as yellowish goo poured from her injured socket. Hugo caught Calla in his arms.

"Say the spell, Abigail!" Endera shouted.

Abigail said the spell one last time, and the netherworld disappeared, replaced by a stinging blackness, and then they were back in the clearing outside Baba Nana's hut. It was nighttime, the air cool and damp. Stars lit up the sky.

Abigail checked to see that they were all there. "We made it," she said, sagging in relief.

"Calla?" Hugo bent over the girl. "Wake up. Say something."

Calla's face was pale as milk. Her eyes were closed. She didn't appear to be breathing.

Abigail glared at Endera. "You let her get bit."

The witchling sneered back. "This is all your fault, Abigail. From now until the day we die, we will be sworn enemies." She rushed off into the woods, followed closely by her pals.

"Endera, wait!" Abigail said.

Baba Nana's voice came from the darkness. "Let her go, child. There's no time. Help me get Calla inside."

Hugo and Abigail lifted the girl and followed Baba Nana into her shack. She cleared off the kitchen table, and they laid Calla on it.

Baba Nana grasped Abigail by the shoulders. "It's up to you, Abigail. Endera will be bringing Melistra back here.

I didn't find anything in the book that can help Calla find her magic, but you can use it to heal her." She held out the spellbook.

Abigail took it hesitantly. "What do you mean?"

Baba Nana nodded at the book in Abigail's hands. "Command the spellbook to give you what you need. Your magic will provide the rest."

Abigail opened the book. The words on the page were a jumble. "I don't know what to do."

"Yes, you do," Hugo said. "Trust your magic."

"What do you know?" Abigail said irritably, wishing it were that simple.

He put a hand on her shoulder. "I know you, Abigail Tarkana. And I know you can do anything you put your mind to."

Abigail took a deep breath and let the spellbook fall open. The words on the page came into focus.

*Try this one, dark witch. You'll like it.*

An icy shiver ran up her spine. For a moment she was tempted, and then she shook it off.

"No. A different spell," she commanded.

The page blew over. She studied the new page. Again, tempting but somehow wrong.

"No! I demand that you give me the spell I need!"

The book riffled through several pages until Abigail suddenly stabbed her finger down on the parchment. The book resisted, as it were fighting her.

She pressed her finger down harder and the words swam into view.

*This one is right.*

She didn't know how she knew it, but it was right. She stood over Calla, putting one hand over the girl's heart as she held the book open.

"*Cora vivina, cara estima, cura malada.*" At her words, a bolt of azure fire shot from her hand into Calla's chest. It was deeper and bluer than any witchfire she had used before.

"What are you doing?" Hugo shouted. "You'll incinerate her!"

"I don't know!" She started to draw her hand back, but Baba Nana grasped her shoulder.

"Don't stop. It's working."

Oddly, Calla didn't seem affected by the powerful witchfire. She lay still and serene as the deep blue fire went into her. Abigail's arm began to shake with the effort. She was getting tired.

"A little longer," Baba Nana said.

"I can't," Abigail cried, feeling her magic running out. Her arms were shaking so badly she dropped the spellbook. One last spark of light went into Calla, and then the witchfire sputtered out. Abigail dropped to her knees, gasping for air.

"Did it work?" she asked.

Hugo put his ear to Calla's heart, listened, then shook his head.

# Chapter 34

Baba Nana wailed. "It has to work. Dear girl." She cradled the limp witchling. "Come back to your Baba Nana."

Abigail pulled herself up and stared at Calla's pale face. What had she done wrong? Why hadn't it worked?

She pushed Baba Nana away and put one hand on Calla's chest. She needed a heartbeat. A solid *thump*. She pressed harder and sent every bit of energy she had into her palm.

*Just one* thump, *Calla.*

*Just one* thump.

Thump.

*Thump.*

Calla gasped as her eyes flew open, and Abigail fell backward.

"What happened?" Calla asked, looking from Baba Nana to Hugo.

"You were bitten by Queen Octonia, but Abigail brought you back," Hugo said, grinning.

Calla blinked, sitting up. "I feel funny."

At that moment the door to the shack flew open, and Melistra stood in the doorway.

"Give me my spellbook," Melistra commanded.

When Abigail hesitated, she shot out her hand, and Abigail clutched at her throat, choking for air. But Baba Nana stepped forward, shedding her pile of rags and drawing herself up to reveal a lean figure that was much taller than she appeared.

"Let the girl alone, Melistra, or you'll have me to deal with." A nasty looking ball of witchfire hovered over one hand. She didn't look anything like the hapless creature they had first seen.

"Balastero. How dare you interfere?" Melistra hissed. "I should have reduced you to cinders years ago. This girl nearly killed my daughter. She will be punished."

"Like you punished Lissandra?" Baba Nana said. "I'm not afraid of you, Melistra. And from now on, I won't be silent. Be warned."

Melistra's eyes widened in shock, then the ice returned to them. "This isn't over."

She snapped her fingers, and the spellbook flew across the room into her hands. In a burst of purple smoke, she vanished.

"What was that about?" Abigail asked.

"Never you mind, child," Baba Nana said. She lifted her cloak of rags and wrapped it around her shoulders, becoming a stooped, huddling figure again.

"Tell me about my mother," Abigail pleaded. "How did she die?"

Pain crossed Baba Nana's face. "It was a terrible night. She was running away from the Tarkanas for good, taking you with her."

"Why would she leave the coven?"

"Her time with Rigel changed her. She was ordered to leave you in the Creche and resume her role in the coven, but she couldn't bear to be separated from you. So, she left. She hadn't gotten far when that vicious creature attacked her in the woods."

"A viken?" Hugo asked.

Baba Nana looked surprised. "How do you know of the viken?"

"One of them has been after me," Abigail said, "ever since I got to the Tarkana Fortress."

Baba Nana snorted. "It must have your scent from that night in the woods. It was Melistra that created it. She got her hands on some old spellbooks from her ancestor, Vena Volgrim. She released it that night when your mother fled with you. I couldn't prove she did it."

"Why would she do that?" Abigail asked.

Baba Nana's eyes slid away. "My guess is she thought your mother was a traitor."

There was something Baba Nana wasn't telling them.

"Then why did you get banished?" Abigail asked.

"Because I was her instructor. I taught Advanced Beasts to the acolytes who showed promise. Melistra was my star pupil. She told the High Witch Council the viken was my creation—that I had set it free. She claimed not to have the magic to do such a thing. She was clever enough to hide Vena's journals in my chambers. The only good news is they were destroyed."

"What happened to the viken?" Hugo asked.

"We searched for it, but it was never found. I think Melistra hid it somewhere out in the swamps."

"Baba Nana," Calla whispered.

"What is it, child?"

"Look."

Calla held out her hand. She trembled as she turned her palm over. On top of it hovered a tiny spark of witchfire. "I've got my magic!"

# Chapter 35

After they exchanged goodbyes and promises to return to visit, it was time to head home. Calla was practically bursting to tell everyone she had her magic.

They started walking down the road to the Tarkana Fortress. Moonlight lit their way, and for the first time in weeks, Abigail wasn't afraid of a rabid beast jumping out of the bushes at them.

"Thanks," Calla said, linking her arm with Abigail's. "If I didn't say it before, you're a true friend."

"I couldn't have done it without Hugo," Abigail said, linking arms with him.

"For a Balfin, he's quite all right," Calla teased.

They all laughed, gravel crunching underfoot as they crossed onto the path that led to the side gate into the gardens.

"That's odd," Abigail said, frowning. "Someone left the gate open."

"Maybe Endera came this way," Calla said.

They entered the gardens and stood under the jook-berry tree.

"I should get home," Hugo said, "before my parents send out a search party."

He turned to go, but Abigail put her hand on his arm, stilling him.

It was quiet. Too quiet.

As if all the night animals had vanished.

"I feel it too," he said softly.

"What do you suppose it is?" Calla whispered.

Out of the darkness, a beast landed in the middle of the clearing, planting its massive paws in the earth, spraying them with dirt and gravel.

The viken opened its jaws and brayed a thunderous growl.

Abigail screamed, taking a step back. "I thought you took care of it."

'I did," Hugo said, "It must have escaped the bog somehow."

Abigail threw a solid blast of witchfire. It hit the viken in the shoulder, making it roar in pain.

Calla joined in, lobbing tiny spurts. "What should we do?" she asked.

"Run!" Abigail said.

They fled down the path, with the viken only steps behind. Abigail kept turning, flinging witchfire at its slavering jaws. It slowed the viken but didn't stop it.

They entered the courtyard and raced toward the Great Hall.

Just a few more steps and they would be inside.

A flash of green burst at Abigail's feet, sending her spinning. Someone had shot witchfire at her. She watched from the ground, dazed, as Hugo and Calla reached the top of the steps before realizing she wasn't with them.

"Abigail!" Hugo shouted.

The beast landed on her. Tearing pain ran up her arm as its claws grazed her skin. Warm blood soaked her uniform. She called up a ball of witchfire, shoving it in the viken's mouth. It howled, spitting it out to the side, and roared in her face, spraying her with spittle.

A figure hurtled onto its back. Hugo tried to wrestle it off Abigail.

"Get off her, you filthy animal!"

The viken tossed its head back, sending Hugo tumbling across the cobblestones. But the distraction had given Abigail time to get to her feet.

She weaved slightly, feeling light-headed. As the beast leapt at her, she called out the only spell that could save her.

"*Gally mordana, gilly pormona, gelly venoma.*"

The viken froze midair, held in place by the spell. A frightened look came into its eyes as its body shimmered and shook. It pawed frantically, trying to reach Abigail, and then it vanished in a wash of cold air.

Abigail was about to help Hugo up, when a sudden movement caught her eye.

Melistra stepped out from behind a pillar, her face a mask of rage. She raised her hand, holding a ball of witchfire, preparing to send it at Abigail, when light spilled out of the Great Hall. Melistra retreated into the shadows as Madame Vex rushed out, followed by several other teachers shouting out questions.

Abigail tried to explain, but a wave of dizziness hit her, and she sank into oblivion.

# Chapter 36

Abigail woke to late-afternoon sunlight streaming through her attic room window. She winced at the pain in her arm. Pulling the blanket away, she found bandages covering the deep scratches the viken had left. Someone had applied a pungent ointment and wrapped her wounds in gauze. She sat up and nearly choked in surprise.

Madame Vex sat at the end of her bed, back ramrod straight.

"Glad to see you're alive," the headmistress said. She poured a glass of water from a pitcher and passed it to Abigail.

She took a long sip, unsure what to say.

"You are reckless," Madame Vex went on in her crisp voice. "We nearly lost three witchlings because of it. But you protected the coven from that vicious creature, so you won't be expelled. You will, however, lose your Head Witchling pin as punishment for sending Endera and the others to the netherworld."

She held out her hand.

Abigail picked up her rumpled uniform and unpinned the gold *T*, handing it over.

Madame Vex stood. "When you recover, I expect you to resume your studies and catch up on any missed work."

"Thank you, Madame Vex, for letting me stay."

The headmistress paused at the door. "I had a dear friend a long time ago. You remind me quite a bit of her."

"Who was she?"

"Her name was Lissandra. She was a foolish girl, always had her head in the clouds. In the end, she forgot what was important."

"What's that?"

Madame Vex turned, pinning her with blazing eyes. "The coven, Abigail. Don't make her mistake. The coven will protect you. The coven is your family."

Madame Vex went out and shut the door.

Abigail flopped back, remembering the viken's horrid breath and its wicked teeth so close to her throat.

She needed fresh air. Rising, she dressed gingerly, slipping her sea emerald around her neck and adding two more items to her pockets. She wandered the garden paths until she found herself under the jookberry tree. Thoughts chased through her head as she stared up at the clouds. As the sun dropped lower, the sky darkened, and a star appeared. It hung low, twinkling a familiar blue.

"Hello, Father," she whispered. "I don't even know you, but I miss you."

She tried to imagine what he was doing right now. What did a star feel?

"They feel quite a lot in Rigel's case."

The calm voice came from the woman beside her.

Vor.

Once again, the Goddess of Wisdom was seated on the

grass, quietly picking daisies. Fireflies danced around her head, creating a warm halo.

"Vor!" Abigail sat up. "I'm so glad to see you. Did you know my father?"

Vor gave a delicate shrug. "I knew of him. He was special to Odin. Thor was a favored son, and Rigel—he was known as Aurvandil then—was a big help to Thor. He earned Odin's gratitude."

Abigail looked back at the star. "I wish I could talk to him."

"Words have power when spoken from the heart. They can even reach the stars." She was silent, and then her voice dropped. "Have you considered Odin's offer of sanctuary?"

"Yes." Abigail looked into Vor's milky eyes, gathering her courage. "How do I know he wouldn't use me as a pawn as well?" she blurted out.

Vor smiled, looking pleased. "Good. You are learning. The answer is you don't, of course. That is why the choice is so difficult."

Abigail sighed, making up her mind. "I can't leave. I'm sorry. I am a Tarkana witch. My coven must come first."

A flicker of sadness passed over Vor's face. "I understand." She rose to her feet, gracefully unfolding her limbs. "That means our time together has come to an end."

"Don't go." Abigail hurried to her feet. "There's so much I don't know."

Vor put a hand on her shoulder. "Be mindful, Abigail. You used dark magic when you cast those girls into the netherworld. Its power over you will grow. The more you use it, the more it will draw you in."

A chill wind blew across the clearing. Vor's image began to glow, and then it dissolved into a cloud of fireflies that darted away in the breeze.

Abigail looked back at the sky. The blue star continued to glitter brightly. "What am I to do, Father? You told me to trust my heart. Was I wrong?"

There was a scuffling sound and a red berry fell on her head. She looked up to see Hugo grinning from the branches. He dropped down to land next to her.

"I didn't think you would be here," he said. "Are you okay?"

"Just a little sore. Melistra was there. In the courtyard. She's the one who tripped me."

"I know. I saw her. Look." He pulled out his notebook and thumbed to the page where he had copied Fetch's note to Odin. "The dark one rises. Do you think it could mean Melistra?"

"It might. It would mean Odin is worried about what she can do." She turned to look at the fortress.

*Or is he worried about something I can do?* she wondered silently, remembering how the spellbook had called her dark witch.

"I have something for you," she said, turning to Hugo. She handed him a flashy medallion on a silver chain. "This one's for Emenor. I added some wonkety magic. Just wait until he uses it. His Maths homework just might disappear."

Hugo grinned. "Thanks."

"And this one is for you." She handed him a simple pendant made of black onyx. "I think you'll like the magic I put in it."

His eyes widened. "Really? Are you sure? I don't want you to think I'm using you."

"I don't. I know you love magic as much as I do. Use it, and I'll refill it whenever you want."

"You'd do that for me?"

"Of course. We're friends, right?"

"The best."

He gave her a swift hug and then stepped back, looking embarrassed. "You were talking to your father before, weren't you?"

She nodded and glanced up at the blue star. "Do you think he'll ever come back?"

"He came once. Maybe he'll come again." He studied the sky. "Until then, no matter where you are or what you're doing, think of him watching over you."

Abigail smiled at her friend. She liked that. She liked that very much.

# Epilogue

Endera rapped her knuckles on the door high in the tower. Her knees were knocking together so hard she was bound to have bruises.

"Come in."

Her heart hitched at the stern sound of her mother's voice. Hands shaking, she turned the knob.

Melistra stood by the fireplace, staring into the flames.

"Mother? You asked to see me?"

"Shut the door."

Endera obeyed, taking two steps into the room.

"Do you have anything to say?" Melistra turned to face her daughter.

Endera hung her head. "I'm sorry. I should have never let Abigail get hold of your spellbook. It won't happen again."

She waited for her mother to scold her, but Melistra was silent. The High Witch stepped closer and tilted Endera's chin up. Her eyes were a fierce green.

"You are my daughter, so I will forgive you this once. Disappoint me again, and I will have no further use for you. Am I clear?"

Endera bit her lip hard to take the wobble out of her voice before she answered.

"Yes, Mother, I will not fail you again." As her mother moved away, she added, "I saw something strange."

Melistra went perfectly still. "What?"

"When Abigail used her witchfire in the netherworld. It was blue for just a moment."

Melistra's eyes flared and she smacked her hands together. "I knew she was Lissandra's child."

"What does that mean?"

Her mother's answer was cryptic. "It means the Rubicus Prophecy has begun. We must act quickly if we are to change the outcome."

She grasped Endera's shoulders.

"From now on, I want a report on everything that mongrel witchling does. You will deliver it to me personally once a week, and I will see to you developing your magic. One way or another, we will destroy that witchling before she ruins this coven."

Endera couldn't stop the smile that crossed her face.

Destroy Abigail? It would be her pleasure.

# THE END

# From the Author

Dear Reader:

I hope you enjoyed *The Blue Witch*! It has been so fun delving into the past of my favorite *Legends of Orkney*™ characters. I love finding out more about Sam Baron's mom, Abigail, and how she got her start at the Tarkana Witch Academy.

As an author, I love to get feedback from my fans letting me know what you liked about the book, what you loved about the book, and even what you didn't like. You can write me at PO Box 1475, Orange, CA 92856, or e-mail me at author@alaneadams.com. Visit me on the web at www.alaneadams.com and learn about starting a book club with my *Legends of Orkney*™ series or having me visit your school to talk about reading!

I want to thank my son Alex for inspiring me to write these stories, and his faith in me that I would see them through. To my wonderful editor, Jennifer Silva Redmond, thank you for pointing out all my many flaws! To my amazing foundation director, Lauri, a million thanks for your willingness to do read-alouds with me again and again. And of course a big shoutout to the team at Spark-Press for their unfailing support. Go Sparkies!

Look for more adventures with Abigail and Hugo as they try to learn more about her past in *The Rubicus Prophecy* coming Fall 2019.

To Orkney! Long may her legends grow!

—Alane Adams

# About the Author

Alane Adams is an author, professor, and literacy advocate. She is the author of the Legends of Orkney fantasy mythology series for tweens and *The Coal Thief, The Egg Thief, The Santa Thief* picture books for early-grade readers. She lives in Southern California.

*Author photo © Melissa Coulier/Bring Media*

# SELECTED TITLES FROM SPARKPRESS

SparkPress is an independent boutique publisher delivering high-quality, entertaining, and engaging content that enhances readers' lives, with a special focus on female-driven work. Visit us at www.gosparkpress.com

*The Thorn Queen,* Elise Holland, $16.95, 9781943006793. Twelve-year-old Meylyne longs to impress her brilliant, sorceress mother—but when she accidentally breaks one of Glendoch's First Rules, she accomplishes the opposite of that. Forced to flee, the only way she may return home is with a cure for Glendoch's diseased prince.

*The Red Sun,* Alane Adams. $17, 978-1-940716-24-4. After learning that his mom is a witch and his missing father is a true Son of Odin, twelve-year-old Sam Baron must travel through a stonefire to the magical realm of Orkney on a quest to find his missing friends and stop an ancient curse.

*Wendy Darling Vol 1: Stars,* Colleen Oakes. $17, 978-1-94071-6-96-4. Loved by two men—a steady and handsome bookseller's son from London, and Peter Pan, a dashing and dangerous charmer—Wendy realizes that Neverland, like her heart, is a wild place, teeming with dark secrets and dangerous obsessions.

*Kalifus Rising,* Alane Adams, $16.95, 978-1940716848. Sam Baron's attempt to free his father brought war to Orkney. Now captured by the Volgrim witches, Sam's only hope lies with his friends—but treachery shadows their every step.

*The Raven God,* Alane Adams, $16.95, 978-1-943006-36-6. As an army of fire giants amasses in the south, prepared to launch all-out war on the defenseless Orkney, Sam embarks on a rescue mission to bring Odin back from the dark underworld of Helva—but the menacing Loki is pulling all the strings.

# About SparkPress

SparkPress is an independent, hybrid imprint focused on merging the best of the traditional publishing model with new and innovative strategies. We deliver high-quality, entertaining, and engaging content that enhances readers' lives. We are proud to bring to market a list of *New York Times* best-selling, award-winning, and debut authors who represent a wide array of genres, as well as our established, industry-wide reputation for creative, results-driven success in working with authors. SparkPress, a BookSparks imprint, is a division of SparkPoint Studio LLC.

Learn more at GoSparkPress.com